AF253281

Other Books by Ann Birstein

STAR OF GLASS

THE TROUBLEMAKER

THE SWEET BIRDS OF GORHAM

SUMMER SITUATIONS

DICKIE'S LIST

AMERICAN CHILDREN

American Children

ANN BIRSTEIN

AN AUTHORS GUILD BACKINPRINT.COM EDITION

For my own American child,
Cathrael

One

1

Rosalie came off the subway into class approximately twenty-five minutes late, just as Professor Houghton, who had begun the term with Thomas Hardy and worked his way back to Beowulf was saying, "That was good king." Of course, it was a long ride from the Grand Concourse, where Rosalie lived, to Flushing, where she presumably went to school, but that was no excuse. Not that, as usual, Rosalie acted as if she needed one. Plump and bouncy, wobbling in her high-heeled ankle-straps, she blithely crossed the room in front of Professor Houghton's desk and he blinked. "That was good king," Houghton repeated tonelessly. Then he laid down his book and like the rest of us watched her climb over several students to an empty seat in the last row, tug at the ermine hairband askew on her thin dark curls, shrug off her white woolly coat, and then lean forward in a posture of elaborate attentiveness so that the sequins scattered across the bosom of her pink sweater caught the hushed winter sunshine and turned into dazzling pinpoints of light. She was wearing even more makeup than usual, an orangy pancake, and one of her eyes was mascaraed all around in the style of Theda Bara. The other eye was covered with a large black patch. "That was good king," Professor Houghton said for the third time, more firmly but somehow more hopelessly, and we all turned around again. Outside, the campus carolers launched into still another chorus of "God Rest Ye Merry, Gentlemen."

I turned with the rest, I even underlined what I had written in my notebook at the beginning of the hour: "*Dec. 23, 1946, Survey of Eng. Lit., Eng. 402.*" But the sight of that eyepatch had stopped me cold, and good and obedient student though I was, the last twenty minutes of the class were lost on me. I just sat there trying to decide whether to quit being friends with Rosalie forever or not. How *could* she? After all we had been through in the past two and a half years, how *could* she pull that stunt with the eyepatch again? It was a wild wanton risk—and of course typically Rosalie. Which meant, naturally, that far from quitting I would probably remain Rosalie's friend forever. "Empathy," Rosalie called it, having somehow managed to catch a few sessions of Professor Polk's Classical Drama I. "The role of a girlfriend is to empathize." In which case, even by Polk's standards, I was perfect for the part, having empathized with Rosalie ever since we had stood on line at freshman registration, a line composed mainly of girls since it was still wartime then, and she had turned around to me, a perfect stranger, waving a crossed-out form and a stumpy pencil in my face and crying, "*You* look sensible. Maybe you know why I'm wasting my life here. Or to come at it another way, maybe *you* know why these harpies require me to rise at six A.M. in the Bronx in order to play volleyball in Queens at eight."

The answer was simple. Medaglia was a city college and freshmen registered last, when all the good classes were already closed. But simple answers in Rosalie's case were as irrelevant as insane solutions were typical, and during this last term alone I had already empathized on the four consecutive occasions when she had overslept for a twelve o'clock class in Abnormal Psychology, missed about ten exams, got penalized for incomplete papers, was suspended from Basketball and Tumbling for wearing long rhinestone earrings with her gym suit. All of which wasn't even to mention the time in Science Survey I when she leaned down to squint at an experiment in her microscope and singed the whole right side of her hair in a Bunsen burner. And somehow—empathy—I was the one who worried about reprisals from the Dean. I was the one who consoled Rosalie's mother when she called in the evening. "No, of course not, Mrs. Golden, naturally I won't say you called. Yes, honestly, Mrs. Golden, there's absolutely nothing to worry about. No, truly, I guarantee your heart won't break."

I stood up, gathering my coat, my books, sighing, trying to be fair. Rosalie worried too—in her special way. With every crisis the lipstick became more purple, the mascara murkier, the sequins and beads blossomed even more profusely and desperately over her curves and bulges, and only the other day I had seen her corner three Turkish exchange students in the cafeteria and try to convince them that Hindemith himself had invited her to study at Yale. Now the eyepatch. "You're asking me *why* do I go through this?" she would say with a bitter laugh. "You're kidding. Because an ironic fate has decreed that I live in the Bronx, that's why. Oh, what's the use? I was born to tragedy."

Tragedy and the Bronx. When Rosalie said these words they sounded like great waves of life breaking through us all.

I pushed my way back to her. She was buttoning up the white woolly coat, which ended somewhere around her ankles. "One more chorus of 'God Rest Ye Merry, Gentlemen,' and I'll puke," she said. "By the way, observe where the comma falls."

"Never mind the aesthetics," I said, pulling her aside as other students squirmed past us. "Punctuation." "Punctuation. Rosalie, have you gone mad? How can you do this to us? You know you can't get away with it twice."

She disengaged my hand gently. "Lois, you're my friend," she said, looking at me with her uncovered eye. "Maybe even my best friend. But please don't presume too much on the basis of our relationship."

"*Presume* too much?"

"Hysteria will get us nowhere," Rosalie said. "I have to get away with it, that's all there is to it. You know as well as I do if I take that test I'll flunk. And you know as well as I do if I flunk what my life is worth."

I nodded drearily and propelled her by the elbow out onto the porch of the English Building, where we stood breathing in the cold winter air. Rosalie's mother had already announced that if she failed one more course she would yank her out of school and send her to work.

"And believe me, she means business this time," Rosalie said. "All day Sunday she sits poring over the want ads. She smells blood, I tell you. '5yrs exp, 40hr wk, $35.' To her it's a king's ransom."

"But Rosalie, be reasonable. You've already pulled this stunt once. You know you can't get away with it again."

"Last time I only said the eye was infected. This time I'm saying I lost it completely."

"Okay, Rosie. And what about afterwards?"

"Afterwards?" Rosalie said, smiling and tripping over her hem as she started down the stairs. "Afterwards I'll gouge it out, if necessary. Anything is better than being a Bronx secretary at nineteen."

We set out across the campus toward the cafeteria. Rosalie kept teetering in those high heels on the icy walks. I was sorry for both our sakes that we were nearing the Christmas holiday, not Easter. In the spring everything, even Rosalie, was sleepier and safer. Trees budded and burgeoned in the agricultural high school next door. People played tennis in their gym suits. Professor Curtis opened the windows during his Wagner I and we all dreamed and fell in love to a scratchy recording of the *Liebestod*. But Christmas was different. I just felt out of it. Rosalie, the opposite. It all called out to her, she said, all of it: the choir rehearsing in the auditorium, the first electric lights burning inside the buildings in the early morning, the silent tangy dusk over the campus when the last class was finished. All of it stirred up strange feelings within her, she said, and as we walked I could believe it. Her head kept turning restlessly, and her body even in that long absurd woolly coat seemed to strain upward with yearning. When we came to the cafeteria she sighed heavily and pushed open the big glass doors.

It was dark noon. Inside there was a sudden great rush of noise, the glint of chromium pillars. We took our places on the slowly shifting food line, with Rosalie shaking her head whenever somebody asked her what happened. A lot of people knew Rosalie at least by sight and a lot laughed whenever they saw her. I never talked to the ones who laughed. Rosalie did if she felt like it. As we shuffled past the glass food cases, Rosalie reached in for a big piece of chocolate cake, changed her mind, and with shoulders drooping settled for a cottage cheese salad and a cup of tea. Our usual crowd was at the usual table, but Rosalie wanted seclusion. We sat down near the steps to the student lounge, I at least, aware of the Turkish exchange students staring at us.

"You didn't ask me why I was all dressed up," Rosalie said.

I hadn't asked because I could never tell. Rosalie often wore sequins to school.

"I'm going to a party later—*if* I get out of that test. It's possible some important show people will be there. I'm going alone."

She waited a moment and I smiled to hide my discomfort. Rosalie was not popular in the usual sense—

she laughed at girls who were—but I knew it hurt her feelings to have to go to parties alone. She would sit glittering nervously in her beads and bangles and rhinestones, and if I was there, toward the end of the evening she would beckon to me with a long cigarette holder and tell me all the guests were Philistines, especially the boys.

"And why shouldn't I go alone?" Rosalie said. "Is it more humiliating than going home on the D?" She lifted her fork to the cottage cheese and set it down again. "You think I'm obsessed."

"Well, not exactly obsessed so much as—" I looked yearningly at our usual table. They were all there: Gerald, Robby Wilson, Milton Schwartz, Leonora Edleman, Luke Lazar, Betty Rubin, even the sorority girl who was always pathetically trying to get us to join up.

"But even you must see that if I didn't live in that accursed borough my whole life would be different. Take even the most fundamental thing, like who ever heard of a nightclub singer who lives in the Bronx? Okay, some of them do rise from obscure origins, I agree. But what chanteuse in history was still in the Bronx when fame overtook her?"

"I don't know," I said, looking over at the table again. Leonora Edleman was holding forth. Gerald was laughing and eating.

"But you're not sure. You believe it's theoretically possible to stay home and still achieve my destiny"— she held up her hand—"and I agree. That is, I'd agree if I lived alone. By myself I could thrive in a rathole.

But as long as my mother is with me, I'm doomed. You know that."

She wasn't being fair. Milton Schwartz over there lived in the Bronx too, with an older sister Myrna as well as a widowed mother, and he never complained. Also Rosalie's mother actually wasn't as bad as some. I mean we all had mothers.

"You hesitate. You like her," Rosalie said, while I finished up my tuna fish sandwich, saving the potato chips. "You're charmed by that musky Russian émigré voice. You're impressed by her penchant for buying teacups on the Grand Concourse and mounting them to look like relics from a Czarist past. You admire the fact that she works in an artificial-flower factory all day long and then comes home and floats real roses in the centerpiece. . . . No, don't deny it. If she weren't my mother I'd admire her too. She's a great lady, straight out of Tolstoy. Everything she does is sensational, great theater. But it's meant to be looked at from the balcony, not lived with. These scenes every day are killing me."

Rosalie sipped from her teacup, leaving a purple imprint on the rim. "Did I tell you her latest? Even if I don't flunk out, she wants me to give piano lessons at night. Can you imagine me teaching scales to the local urchins? I, whom Hindemith himself invited to study at Yale?" She looked at me one-eyed and anxious, brushing at the sweaty curls that had fallen free of the ermine band. "Anyway, it's all bigger than the sum of its parts. Don't you ever yearn for freedom, even vaguely?"

"I already live in Manhattan."

"With your parents," Rosalie pointed out, and then lost interest. "Anyway, for myself I can assure you that I wasn't meant to sit here eating cottage cheese and failing Science Survey I. I was meant to stand in a spotlight. Sing! Dance! Bring people joy!" She had thrown up her arms and her bracelets clanged together. Nobody at our regular table was watching her, but the Turkish exchange students remained transfixed.

"Rosie," I said, "maybe it would be better if you left school right now."

"And have her slap me into an office job? Never." She lowered her arms. "All I ask is for her to lend me enough money to rent an apartment of my own. In Manhattan. Midtown."

"There aren't any apartments. And what if she can't?"

"Then it's simple. For the rest of my life I'll sink deeper into despair. Trapped and doomed."

"Look," I said, "you're going to have the whole vacation off soon. You can make up your work. Things will get better."

We both knew I was lying and she smiled at me patiently, as at a prattling child.

"Not better, worse," she said in an ominously quiet voice. "We still don't know if I'll get out of that test today." She stood up and engulfed herself in the long woolly coat, waving away the sorority girl who had just been waved away by Leonora. "In fact I told her last night that if things went on this way I'd definitely kill myself."

"And she said?" I asked, knowing the answer already.

"She said she'd kill herself first and make a fool out of me."

"Rosalie," I said, standing up too as the bell rang. "I think you exaggerate. You and your mother both. You act as if you were in a Greek tragedy or something."

Rosalie fumbled with her eyepatch and set it straight. Then she squared her woolly shoulders. "Greek tragedy was *domestic* tragedy," Rosalie said. "Remember that."

2

The ringing of the change-classes bell had raised the noise level in the cafeteria several hundred decibels and caused new crowding and shifting on the food line. I dumped my coat and pile of books at the regular table, waving at Gerald, and went to get some more coffee, glad to be rid of Rosalie for a while and guilty about it. When I came back, most of the usual guard were still there, surrounded by the litter of their lunches, and I suddenly wondered what made us a group. Not Rosalie, who couldn't be said to belong anywhere, except maybe with Luke Lazar, who sometimes wrote routines for her and was now struggling with his Spanish dictation, but the rest. Gerald Muster, I thought, trying to characterize them, an aspiring tenor.

Milton Schwartz, an aspiring painter. Also, Robby Wilson, serious English major, Betty Rubin, former president of her high school G.O. and the only one among us who might possibly be called a coed, Maria Gato, who never seemed to leave the cafeteria at all, but sat there dolefully like a mater dolorosa—I wasn't even sure if she was still registered—Sherwin Schiff, gadfly, Leonora the Weird, so called by Robby not only because she was weird, which in a way she was, but because weird was the kind of word Leonora would use. Also guelph. At fourteen she had read Proust in the original, as she never tired of telling us, at sixteen had her own subscription to *Partisan Review*. Now she was in the middle of a not particularly funny anecdote about meeting Rudolph Serkin's nephew at a concert in Town Hall. And I? No known occupation.

I tuned in on Leonora, who was finishing up. "'Uncle Rudy,' he called him," she said, and laughed. "Isn't that marvelous?"

"*Marvelous*," Sherwin echoed her. Maria smiled as if she were crying, and then belatedly Gerald laughed his usual dopey laugh, tee-hee. Had he got it from a comic strip? Partly, I supposed, it could be explained away as a matter of vocal exercises. His teacher down at the Greenwich Music School demanded some strange ones. But it took a certain kind of person to go tee-hee anyway, and it didn't suit the rest of him. He was just too handsome. Tall, very tall, with lustrous black hair and a beautiful nose and strong chin. These days he wore civvies, now a tweed jacket with hand-stitched lapels and a bow tie, but even in the silly sailor suit I had first seen him in last September when he was being mustered out of the Navy, Gerald had managed to look gorgeous. Milton Schwartz introduced us and we had become friends at once. Platonic friends. Gerald loved the phrase. Either he had just learned it, or it had never happened to him before.

"Well, what's with Hildegard this time?" Leonora asked me. "Or should I say Lord Nelson?"

I pretended not to have heard—nobody could be fed up with Rosalie but me—and continued to smile at Gerald, a little anxiously when he crumpled up the waxed paper from the last of several sandwiches, looked around for more, and stood up. I gave him my bag of potato chips.

"See you at three?" I said.

"Three?"

"It's Monday."

Had he forgotten? On Mondays we always took the bus and subway together as far as Forest Hills, where Gerald changed for the local to 67th Avenue and I stayed on the express to Manhattan. Fridays I usually went all the way down to the Village with him and waited around while he had his lesson. But this week, on account of Christmas, there wasn't going to be any Friday.

"No, darling, today I have a cappella practice," Gerald said. Across the table, Maria watched the two of us with narrowed eyes. Anything that smelled of trouble attracted her, especially between Gerald and me. I looked at her looking up at Gerald, heart-faced, mournful, deliberately seductive, a quivering sensibility.

Bitch. He could have fallen on her like a redwood and that quivering sensibility would have survived it.

"Tomorrow, then?" I said.

"Sure," Gerald said cheerfully, heading for the stairs to the student lounge and the music listening room.

"Lois," Robby Wilson said, after a moment. "How can a straight A student like you go around with him? What do you *talk* about?"

"Shut up," I said, looking after Gerald nervously. "About the straight A's."

3

Dr. Lorillard shared an office with Dr. Slavitt, who luckily was on his way out as I came in. He gave me a sardonic look, gathered up his papers and books, and left. Or at least I assumed it was a sardonic look, though it was very hard to tell with him. He was like that in class too, the Principles of Literary Criticism, where he casually referred to essays in our anthology of notable authors as "spider droppings." Nevertheless I knew he regarded me in particular as a Goody Two-Shoes, though I hadn't quite realized to what extent until he said I was just the right person to do a paper on the New Criticism and Robby Wilson explained afterwards what Slavitt thought of the New Criticism. The students he liked were the intellectuals, the ones who had heard of Yvor Winters and Allen Tate even before he attacked them, the refugees like Marcel Mandelbaum, whose poetic muse spoke to him on the GG local, Annelore Grossman who wrote stories about boots coming up the stairs in the middle of the night, and of course Leonora Edleman with her Proust in the original. The rumor was that besides being tired-looking Dr. Slavitt was an actual card-carrying Communist, which was hard to believe since he was so strict, so almost patrician in his tastes and standards. Much stricter and more patrician than Dr. Lorillard, who smiled at me interestedly and courteously when I came in. We all knew she couldn't stand Slavitt, not on account of his politics—she was probably as much what my father would have called a fellow traveler as anyone on the faculty—but on account of his boorish manners. Still, she never gave the slightest sign what torture it must have been to share an office with him. In fact she never gave the slightest sign about many things—which was what finally made it dawn on me she was a lady—much the same in class and out, though in an opposite way from Slavitt, curiously elliptical in her speech, with her fair hair cut in a boyish bob, no makeup except a little lipstick, little pearl earrings, and an unexpectedly friendly gap between her front teeth when she smiled. Even that time we caught her having a drink by herself down at Joey's Tavern, she was still exactly the same.

I had come to leave off the outline for my term paper, *The Humor of Character in Charles Lamb's Essays of Elia,* which was due right after Christmas vacation.

"I know it's sketchy," I said, "but I didn't want the bare bones of the skeleton to show through."

She glanced at it, nodded, and handed it back to me. A little white lie—the actual paper would be okay and in on time—but it had been received with too much grace. Didn't even Rosalie feel contrition at such moments?

"I'm sure it will be fine."

"Thank you."

"Maybe you'll want to do your honors on him next year."

"I probably won't even get honors."

"Oh, you will, you will," she said, understanding immediately. "Did you have any other ideas?"

"Maybe Middle English vowel shifts. Though I'm terrible at the physiology."

"Dr. Houghton." The gap-toothed smile faded a bit, but not by much. She had failed to sell her specialty, but it wasn't her real specialty—actually she was a Renaissance man, but in Medaglia everybody doubled in brass—and her mind had gone on to other things. She was reaching into the bottom drawer of her desk and taking out her big teacher's pocketbook. She withdrew a compact and in a surprisingly intimate gesture started to powder her nose—"I always fix up to meet my seminar"—then a little tortoiseshell comb which she ran through her pale boyish bob, patting it here and there. "Baby fine," she explained, smiling broadly again. "Baby fine. I have to keep it this short."

The conference, as much of one as there could be

said to have been, was clearly over, but I hung around, unsure whether it was up to me to formally end it.

"Well, Merry Christmas," Dr. Lorillard said.

I hesitated. "Happy holiday to you too."

"You must come to dinner one night," Dr. Lorillard said, putting away her comb and compact and helping herself into a bunny fur coat.

"Oh, I'd love to."

She picked up her briefcase and smiled again. "You were the only one who chose him, you know."

"I was?"

I followed her out, suffering from a vision of Dr. Slavitt behind me at his empty desk, like acute indigestion. A course in English Prose and Poetry of the Romantic Age. What had been some of the other topics listed on the blackboard to choose from? Shelley's Swoon. Sensuous Imagery in Keats. Byron as Romantic Hero. I could hardly remember. But I, and only I naturally, had picked *The Humor of Character in Charles Lamb's Essays of Elia.*

4

I went down the hall, where our local specialist on Walt Whitman sat in his cubicle with the door open, the only full professor in the department, a round-headed gentleman with pince-nez and cheeks puffing out of a Hoover collar. It was so hard to tell from the looks of people what they specialized in. Then I started down the hill for the bus to take me to the subway, backtracking on impulse to the Administration Building, where the auditorium was. Not a real auditorium, just a kind of empty ballroom with a stage, where folding chairs were set up when the occasion warranted it, assemblies, chapels, convocations, concerts. The Christmas concert would not be until tomorrow, and so the a cappella chorus on stage was singing away to no one, extra lustily conducted by Professor Curtis because, it being a cappella—as I had learned from Gerald—there was no orchestra. Actually, it wouldn't have mattered if there were an orchestra or not. I couldn't hear them. I was outside on the porch, looking in. Gerald was in the back row on account of his height, but he would have been remote anyway. It was all remote. Christmas was already doing that to everything that mattered, even marks. I wished I were a musician. I wished that I could lose myself in the ache and beauty of whatever it was they were singing. I turned away. Maria, that blackbird of misery, had spied me and was coming toward me. The last thing I wanted was for her to find me pressing my nose against the glass where Gerald was and commiserate. I hurried down the icy hill, slipping and sliding almost as badly as poor Rosalie, and caught the bus to the subway just in time, although the other last thing I wanted was to go home.

5

The apartment felt empty, though of course my mother
was there, following the new maid around and check-
ing for dust with an index finger. The new maid was
scared of me. They were always scared of me, mainly
because every time one came from the agency, which
now that the war was over was fairly often, my mother
would say, "*This* is the one you have to please, not
me." It made her the good one, which was not only un-
true, but absolutely ridiculous. What did I care about
cooking, pots and pans, furniture polish, dirty laundry,
garbage? Anybody could have seen that my whole natural milieu was term papers, anthologies, introductions,
notes, *The Humor of Character in Charles Lamb*. She
had missed the point, as usual. But why did it make me
so furious? Why did I always kind of wink at the maid
and smile, as if to say, listen, this woman is a crazy liar.
"American children," which was another infuriating
thing my mother always said.

I wandered around, still thinking about school, but
not wanting to start on any assignments just yet. My
brother Walter's room was genuinely dark and deserted. The furniture, desk, daybed, drawing easel,
stood waiting for him to come back. He was still in the
Army, poor man. Sometimes when he had a pass, I
would wake up at night to find him sitting on the edge
of my bed, wanting to talk. Sometimes he even asked

me out to dinner, like a date. I had once made the mistake of telling Leonora about this, and I was still sorry. She had made fun of it as she made fun of everything, though actually in this case I thought she was mostly jealous, being so madly in love with her own brother, Martin. ("Utterly Thomas Mann, my dear," Sherwin Schiff said.) I didn't blame her. At one time I could have fallen in love with Martin myself if Leonora had only let me get at him. But she guarded him like a lion. One of the lions in front of the Forty-second Street library. Why was I always having to make jokes to myself to get out of being afraid of Leonora?

There was nothing of interest for me in the mail on the drop-leaf table in the foyer. If there had been, my mother would have abstracted it long ago, poring over it at the window, holding it until I had read whatever she wanted me to read to her first. But Robert and his flecked Cornell stationery with the crest had been heard from earlier in the week—he was coming in for Christmas, we were going to have dinner with his sister and her boyfriend at the White Turkey Inn—and the only other possible thing of interest was a letter I couldn't read anyway. A blue envelope thin as tissue paper, addressed in a spidery blue script. Inside it would be written in Yiddish, a language I could understand a little, having heard it ever since childhood whenever my parents didn't want me to understand, but could hardly speak. The first letter had come about six months ago, and I had carried it to my father, who seemed wryly amused that *I* should be acting the immigrant. "My name is Josef," my father had translated

in a curiously unmoved voice, "I am the only one left."
I had expected him to spring into action at once. The
return postmark was a DP camp in Bari, Italy. But no.
Six months had passed, and still the return postmark
was a DP camp in Bari, Italy. I couldn't understand it.
Here was this man, my father, who was so Jewish that
I still found myself saying "Happy Holiday" instead of
"Merry Christmas" to Dr. Lorillard. Here was Manny
Ackerman, such a big shot in the dress business, such a
string puller, that already, though the war had been
over only a year and a half, we owned a new black
Buick, a television console with a tiny flickering screen
the size of a snapshot, incredibly hard-to-come-by bot-
tles of scotch and Canadian Club. So why couldn't he
pull a few more strings and get his own nephew over
here? I didn't understand it, though to be honest, it
was just one of lots of things I was beginning not to understand. Was this the daddy whose lap I used to climb
on, whose cheek I used to kiss, who patiently inter-
ceded between my mother and me, ostensibly on her
side, but actually on mine? *Josef Ackerman.* A cord-
wood corpse I had seen in those horrible newsreels
come to life. My corpse. My family. My own cousin.
My expiation. With his last name the same as mine. In
the beginning Rosalie had pointed out that I could
marry him and retain my own personal identity. That
maybe fate had washed him to shore for me. I wrote a
few letters of my own and got a few back, one of them
containing a small photograph of a young man who
vaguely resembled an early version of my father.
"What else?" Rosalie asked. I hesitated. "He says he

weighs seven stone and that his eyes are beer-colored." Rosalie and I looked at each other. "It's possible that when you do meet, you'll understand each other perfectly," Rosalie said.

My father came home from Lowyse Frocks, saying nothing about his business, as usual, not that I ever asked him, and my mother bustled in and out of the kitchen, wearing a flowered wrap apron over her good dress. The maid, of course, wore a small white doily over a black uniform. Finally, we sat down to dinner at the foyer table, leaves now extended and swept clear of ornamental ashtrays, snake plant, mail, including Josef's letter, and at which, after my mother had looked at me and then shaken her little bell, the maid walked around serving kosher pot roast from the left. Nervously when she got to me. I was the one to please. My father made a joke about sugar rationing with her over his shoulder and she smiled.

"What did Josef say this time?" I asked as we were finishing up the canned fruit salad.

"Nothing." My father tossed his napkin aside, and headed for the living room and his television set. In my house, nobody ever seemed to say please or thank you very much, even in spite of the scurrying maid and the little bell. Least of all my father, that self-made man and proud of it, whose proudest boast of all was how he had had to put lead in his pants to qualify for his first working papers and even then hardly made it. He was sitting sunk down on the couch, watching the tiny flickering square of life on the television screen when I came between them. Wrestlers.

"But he must have said *something*," I said. My father waved me away and then tried to see around me. "But, Daddy—"

"He thinks if he could marry an American girl he could come over right away. All right?"

"What's wrong with that?"

My father, intent on the writhing bodies, didn't bother to answer. I stepped back. Still silence.

"You think he means me?"

"I said I didn't want to talk about it."

"But what's so terrible? Especially after everything he's suffered. Anyway, it's just a technicality. After all, Auden married Erika Mann." I wondered why I was talking in the voice of Leonora to make a point she probably wouldn't even have understood.

"I suffered too," my father said. "And I also waited my turn to come to this country."

"Daddy, that was thirty-five years ago!"

"It makes no difference," my father said. "I waited my turn."

My mother came in, untying her apron, and looked at each of us anxiously. She patted my father's gray fringe and when he shook her off, sat down next to him anyway.

"And I had nobody, believe me," my father said. "Stop it, Celia. No uncle trying his best."

"But, Daddy—" My mother nodded. A useless conversation.

I went off to my room, prepared to attack Charles Lamb, and took out some airmail stationery instead.

"My dear cousin, Josef, again I'm sorry that this

must be in English. But as I've confessed before, I don't know much Yiddish and can't write it at all." What else should I confess? That I had learned in Linguistics not to call it Jewish? (*Germanic language, part of the Indo-European family, though written in Semitic characters.*) That Manny Ackerman, that great family man, inexplicably didn't seem to give a damn about his own nephew? That my mother had no mind of her own in anything, so not to look in that direction? I had already told him that I was of medium height with dark hair and blue eyes, a junior at the university (it sounded better, more European than "college"), a university that he too might be interested in attending, that I was nineteen years old but still not sure what I wanted to do, maybe reconstruction work in Europe.

"When I think of what you have been made to suffer, what you must be suffering now, I am deeply ashamed. But at least before long you will be with us. I promise that when you are I will do everything in my power to make you happy. . . ."

How? Concerts, plays, trips to museums? Something was wrong. It was like writing to a deaf person. I began to wonder why I hadn't already heard from Rosalie or, more probably, her mother, and whether this meant good news or bad. But when the phone rang it was first Luke Lazar, mired in the rhyme scheme of a Shakespearean sonnet—"AB, AB," I told him, "CD, CD. Keep your chin up." He hadn't heard from Rosalie either—and then, the last person I wanted to hear from, as well she knew, Maria Gato.

"What do *you* want?"

Her voice was hushed, crushed, furtive. "You're being cruel."

"I am not being cruel. What do you want?"

"I found a room."

By now her voice had sunk to such a conspiratorial whisper that I half looked around to see who was listening in on my side. Which was ridiculous. Maria was always looking for a room, not, like Rosalie, in order to leave home completely, but only on a part-time basis. "You know I'm desperate," she said, and went on with her usual litany of desperation. She was desperate to get away from her mother for just a little while, though Mrs. Gato was a dark cheery little lady whose main sin seemed to be that she had no interest in Lotte Lehman but loved cooking spaghetti. (What did these girls want in their mothers anyhow?) She was desperate for just a modicum of privacy. She was getting desperate about everything. Also, it being Maria, probably the stealth of it appealed to her.

"Where's this one?"

"Eighth Street," Maria said.

Eighth Street? Gerald's music lessons were on Barrow.

"What have I got to do with it?"

"I thought you might want to share—since you're down there so much."

"You're crazy."

"It's only forty dollars a month. We could swing it easily between us."

Forty dollars a month. I *could* swing it, though not easily since it would mean parting with most of my allowance, but—I thought of Rosalie asking me if I didn't yearn for freedom even vaguely, and what an irony it would be if I got there first. I caught myself in time. Share a room with Maria? Was *I* crazy? I automatically repeated that I was *not* being cruel, hung up, and when the phone rang again it was—Gerald.

"Oh, hi," I said, leaning back on my sofa bed. "*Hi.*" Again, not unusual. Gerald often called to chat, even when we had just said goodbye on the subway. In a way this made him more like a girlfriend than a boyfriend, though of course except in the literal sense he wasn't my boyfriend either.

"Merry Christmas. You should have hung around for the a cappella choir," Gerald said.

"Oh, I'll hear the whole thing tomorrow," I said, toying with the cord.

"What are you doing?"

"Writing a paper on Charles Lamb. What are you doing?"

"Practicing my Poulenc. I think I'm in love," Gerald said.

My heart beat so fast I almost choked on it. It was like that last moment before an exam.

"Anybody I know?"

"Maybe."

"Know well?"

"Maybe." Gerald laughed, tee-hee.

"Tell me more."

But Gerald wouldn't. He talked some more about the Poulenc, and then began to outline a production he had in mind of *Pelléas and Mélisande,* singing me snatches as he went along. He was always outlining future productions of operas and recitals, featuring himself as tenor. "Mes longues cheveux descendent jusq'au seuil de la tour, mes cheveux vous attendent tout le longue de la tour, et tout le longue du jour, et tout le longue du jour. . . ." Gerald's in love, I thought, listening to the French, not his singing voice, Gerald's in *love.*

6

I saw him only briefly the next day. From the rear of the auditorium, which was packed with all of us on chairs now. He was all robed and singing away with the a cappella choir, still in the back row on account of his height. Christmas didn't bother him. He wasn't Jewish. "Christmas is coming, the goose is growing fat, please to put a penny in the old man's hat," Gerald sang, and then after a brief wave goodbye—he was going South to visit his mother's family—was off with the other Christians. I hung around, seeking to drum up a conversation, some human companionship, even with Sherwin Schiff, and finally went home by myself. It was a lonely holiday. I had other papers besides the one on Charles Lamb, including *Hypercorrectness in the English Language,* and I went to Room 315 in the New York Public Library to work on them, all dressed up in high heels, my Persian-lamb coat, and a hat with a veil because the rule was that students couldn't use the stacks. There I saw, similarly attired, about four other girls from Medaglia, also working on term papers, also trying to look older. I didn't understand the rule. Who needed books more than students? But then I hated libraries anyway. They were so silent, musty, reproachful, run by elderly ladies with fat and flabby forearms who were always telling you why you couldn't take something out. Each day I was glad to be finished and outside again, though the streets were slippery with gray muck, and the department-store windows full of Christmas. What else? Still no sign of Rosalie. Several times I picked up the phone, remembered what she had said about presuming too much, and put it down again. There was also a card from Gerald postmarked Miami, which surprised me since when he said "mother's family" I had imagined Georgia at least, or South Carolina. The message was illiterate and mainly incomprehensible, something about Alice and the Red Queen, but that didn't matter. I reread it constantly and kept it in my pocketbook, not however showing it to Robby Wilson when we went to the Planetarium and had malteds afterwards. Dutch. I insisted. There was a new funny look in his eye. Nor did I show it to Leonora Edleman when I followed her on foot as she rode her expensive bike, as hard to come by these days as my father's Buick, up and down Central Park West, and then went up to her apartment to sit with her for a while and thaw out. I did of course manage to expose Robert's letter with the crest.

It was a blue winter afternoon. I had been there almost a half hour and it was clear that her brother Martin wasn't around. Which was too bad. I had gotten over my crush on him as a sophomore, when I first saw him in his Air Force uniform, but I still always half hoped he'd show up. It really wasn't much fun visiting Leonora otherwise. She was too, not rich exactly, but awfully well-to-do. Her bedroom had been furnished especially for her, not, like mine and Rosalie's, with castoffs from other parts of the apartment, and contained a vanity table and also twin beds with matching powder blue spreads so that her friends could sleep over. She had shoe bags in her closet. A pair of gray suede pumps, when I could only afford new black ones. She had dresses made of brown velvet with lace collars that were too young for her and therefore seemed more expensive than if they had been too old. In the living room, where Leonora and I sat slumped on the sofa looking out at the view of a bleak park, an elaborately decorated Christmas tree stood in the corner near the grand piano, and over the fireplace hung a pair of pastel portraits of "the children when they were small." The father, a furrier, who supported this establishment, was very nice and hardly ever around, and when he did appear was called "Izzy" by all three of them, Martin, Leonora, and Mrs. Edleman. Mrs. Edleman, who now joined us, looked like Gerald's mother, in spite of the difference in religion, tall, dark, with an upsweep, ankle-strap shoes and, even indoors, an evident affinity for silver fox. I couldn't quite understand why she so clearly disliked me, though she was polite enough, and asked me questions about my grades and school and so on. But what truly puzzled me the longer I sat there was why Leonora went to Medaglia. True that it was the best of the free city colleges. True that Martin had gone there first, five years ago when it was new and small and worthy of him. But Medaglia was no longer select. It was growing, burgeoning, sprawling like the rest of us. Also, Leonora had, in fact, been away to college—Gorham—and then suddenly come back to New York and entered Medaglia in the middle of her sophomore year. "Leonora didn't feel very well," Mrs. Edleman had explained once, with a smile, voluntarily, "and we wanted her close to us so that we could take better care of her." But Leonora hadn't looked sick then and still didn't, but healthy as a horse in fact, with something of the build of a horse, or cow maybe, in spite of the long blond Alice in Wonderland hair streaming down her back from a black velvet hairband. I suppose that the real trouble was that besides adoring Martin, imitating Martin, doing her best to keep Martin away from her friends, she also looked like Martin, which was okay for him but not for her. Today she more than ever resembled a female impersonator. Yet, to be fair, there was also a curious tenderness to her. Once, when I slept over, she had suddenly reached across from her bed to mine and shaken my hand in the dark. Another time, she had brought me a little bottle of violet perfume from Canada. Then again she had this strange friendship with Maria, in which Maria, no longer crushed, was superior and caustic, the two of them united by their artistic sensibilities and the fact of being far too intellectual to care about marks.

The afternoon was getting bluer, almost cobalt. In the corner between the fireplace and the piano, the Jewish Christmas tree took on an evening twinkle. I looked away as the maid, in a black uniform with a doily for an apron, cleared the foyer table and set a little bell on it. Soon there would be a big wooden salad bowl with smaller salad bowls to match. Time to go home. It was getting plainer and plainer that I was not being asked to dinner. Still, obstinately, I wanted to stick around a little more in case Martin did come in. Surely he was home for the holidays. I even thought of taking something out of my pocketbook, my compact maybe, and sandwiching it in between the cushion and the arm of the sofa as an excuse for inviting myself back. Then Martin himself suddenly appeared in our midst—evidently he had been somewhere in the back of the apartment the whole time—the absolute and almost shocking spitting image of Leonora, except that he was in a handsome tweed suit, well over six feet. He was very polite, like a princeling, and as usual greeted me cordially, as if he had never laid eyes on me before. He and Leonora made a few private jokes between them, in which I detected overtones of Rudolph Serkin's nephew and subscriptions to *Partisan Review*. Then Martin turned to me and said to her, "She looks rather like Phoebe White, wouldn't you say?" Leonora laughed and agreed. Who was Phoebe White? What was Phoebe White? Was it an insult or a compliment? It was possible I would never know, since, having delivered himself of that statement, Martin pleasantly left the room. Now it really was time to go. Mrs. Edleman retrieved my compact from the crack in the sofa. "I think you forgot this," she said to me, smiling at Leonora.

7

Inevitably, December 31 was the worst day of the year —1946 being, in retrospect, the worst of all years. I had tried to beat the system, first by yielding to it—I set my hair about six hours before Robert was due to pick me up—and then, in curlers, going over my paper on Charles Lamb, which was awful. "*'Dear Reader, I have no ear.'* Perhaps you did not, Charles Lamb, but you had a heart, a heart which . . ."

My mother, naturally, chose to appear in my doorway at that moment, shaking her head over me as if I were sick or dying.

"So tell me," she said, laughing her mirthless laugh, "it will help you to diaper babies better?"

"I have no intention of ever diapering babies."

"Meshugana."

"I am not meshuga, and please leave me alone."

"Why don't you marry him? He's a nice boy."

"I have no intention of ever marrying anybody."

"So what are you wearing?" my mother continued unperturbed.

"My off-the-shoulder black velvet."

"Why not the blouse Papa's partner brought you from Florida?"

"Because it is vulgar and ostentatious and hand-painted, that's why."

"It's vot dey all vearing," my mother said, shrugging, and lapsing into her deepest accent.

"I don't care 'vot dey vearing' and please leave me alone."

"American children."

"You don't know anything about being American *or* a child!" I cried, finally rising from my desk. "You don't know anything about *anything!*" She stood there silent in her flowered housedress. I was too sorry to say I was sorry.

8

We went to the White Turkey, served by waitresses in Colonial costume, who gave us popovers that went flat and smooth as soon as you bit into them. We also had stuffed turkey and a salad with apples in it, very nice and, okay, very American, and Robert was trying very hard to do the right thing, not even gulping at the check, which maybe came to eight dollars apiece, though in the end we couldn't find a taxi but had to take a bus to the New Year's Eve party itself, where unfamiliar couples sat on either side of a darkened room like opposing firing squads. Robert's sister's boy-friend's parents were either out or in hiding. They were quite rich, however, and the apartment besides being further downtown than the Edlemans' also had a concealed Capehart that sent records crashing down a chute instead of dropping on each other. Still, it was a kind of shock after the wit and charm of Robert's letters on the blue-flecked stationery written in the style of S. J. Perelman and with frequent references to Bach, Mozart and Vivaldi, to come face to face with Robert himself. Long nose, glasses, a touch of acne, round shoulders. Of course, I wasn't being fair. If you had to have a date on New Year's Eve, and there was no point fooling myself or screaming at my mother, you did, at least Robert was dependable. Other boys, even ones you had dated all year, tended to disappear suddenly on this night of nights—viz., Gerald in Florida with his mother, not that he would have come under this category—but Robert was dependable, Robert was steadfast, Robert was true. You could always count on him. He was also decent in many other ways. In fact, though to my shame I tended to keep this secret, on principle he wouldn't even belong to a fraternity at Cornell but roomed in a boardinghouse instead, which was more than decent and very brave. All his political and social sentiments were of this high order. On my last birthday he had even made a contribution in my name to the Haganah instead of giving me a regular present. He was even proud of my being smart in school.

We were all drinking blended whiskey and ginger ale and a lot of us were necking. Yet at the stroke of midnight, kissing Robert whose hand was on my dress,

I wasn't thinking about the New Year, nor of 1947, nor even of Gerald, but of Leonora and the Tavern-on-the-Green. We had gone there one balmy night last summer, Robert and his sister and her boyfriend and I, and there was Leonora with a group of handsome young people. She had called out to us laughing, amid the band, and the couples swaying, and the bright Japanese lanterns. It was a shock to see her there, like a word out of context. She introduced us to her date, Jeff Something, whose last name sounded like a famous brand of pumpernickel. Robert knew him slightly, through mutual friends. Jeff went to Harvard. He was on the swimming team. Robert went to Cornell. He was on the swimming team. There all resemblance ended. Jeff was blond and handsome, the obvious scion of some fortune, pumpernickel or not, so superior and assured it didn't even occur to him to snub us. Later, in the rocky self-service elevator, necking with Robert whose hand was now inside my dress, I kept thinking, why aren't you Jeff? Why aren't there Japanese lanterns and swaying summer songs when *you* pass by? It wasn't fair. Leonora wasn't the least bit beautiful. She wasn't even pretty. It wasn't *fair*. Of course, it wasn't fair to Robert either, but by then I no longer cared. We were at my door and the hand inside my dress was getting too pleasurable. I forcibly sent him home, not to his surprise, he seemed surprised I hadn't done it sooner, and as I unlocked the door, heard my mother scurrying away in the darkness from where she had been watching us through the peephole.

9

I was wrong. New Year's Day was even worse than New Year's Eve. I slept late, made up my sofa bed, had coffee and a bagel in the kitchen, ignoring my father's attempt to ply me with cream cheese and lox, glared at my mother who stood in the doorway in her flowered housedress looking innocent, and then went back to my room to stare out the window at nothing, nothing at all. I had already looked through "The Year in Review" in the *Times*, seen the cartoon of the cheery baby in top hat and diapers chasing off an old man with a sheet and a scythe, considered the problems of postwar unemployment, the returning veteran, the baby boom, peacetime uses of the atom. But for myself all I could foresee was more papers, more homework, more being caught in loveless embraces, until a voice behind me said:

"Happy New Year."

I wheeled around. "Rosalie!"

She walked in wearing her mother's sealskin coat and a ruby red dress gathered at the hip with a floppy velvet rose, also her mother's. Never mind about the coat. When I saw that dress at high noon, I forgot about myself. It was time to be sensible, even if it meant losing her temporarily. Still, it was hard, my heart had lifted so at the sight of her.

"They didn't believe you about the eye," I said, forcing myself to be firm, to go back to before the vacation. "And you had to take the test."

"That's right."

"And you failed it."

"Probably."

"What do you mean, probably? Look, Rosalie—"

"I mean that of course none of that matters anymore. It's all receded into the past for me."

"What do you mean, receded into the past?"

"Because I've met him," Rosalie said.

"You what?"

"I *met* him!" She threw back her head and laughed exultantly. "At that party—I met *him!*"

"Rosie!" I cried. I ran to her, and we hugged each other so hard one of Rosalie's mother's seams burst. Afterwards, when we had finished crying and were sitting down, she filled in the details. Lousy party, but the moment they saw each other across the room they knew. They had been pulled together by an irresistible force. Her heart had told her at once that here was something extraordinary, this even before she observed that his hair was brushed sideways and spiraling onto his brow as if he were a somewhat taller version of Napoleon, even before she learned that his new quarterly had been mentioned unfavorably in *Time* magazine. Later, he told her that being born and brought up in the South and the conditions he found there were what had impelled him to come to New York and found an avant-garde literary review. He wore a black suede jacket and kept a brush for it in his pocket. He was legally separated, though not yet divorced. He was staying with friends in Brooklyn Heights and had just signed a lease for a furnished apartment in Manhattan.

"But facts don't really describe him," Rosalie said. "We simply knew instinctively that this was it. I suppose that's why it happened so simply and without any fanfare. I never even felt the slightest embarrassment at the Algonquin."

"The Algonquin?"

"He's *extremely* literary. But the point is that I didn't even have a single guilt feeling when he asked the clerk for the room. I wasn't even tempted to twist my graduation ring around. Because that wasn't the point. The point was that it was all perfectly natural and frank, the way real relationships are. . . . Excuse me. Are you shocked?"

"I'm not shocked."

"Because if you suddenly turned bourgeois on me now—"

"I'm not bourgeois."

"—I'm afraid it would seriously come between us. You see as soon as he settles in I'm going to go and live with him, and if you're to remain my confidante, Lois, I'll have to depend on your absolute discretion."

"I'm not shocked," I said.

Rosalie laughed and took out her ridiculously long cigarette holder. "Of course you are," she said, sticking one of my cigarettes in it. "Naturally you are. This isn't the kind of decision you'll be called on to make in your own life. Someday you'll marry an accountant or something and live happily ever after. And that's as it should be. But surely you see how wrong that kind of thing would be for me and how right this is. In terms of freedom and self-expression and opportunity. Smack in the middle of Manhattan?"

"I'm not marrying an accountant."

"You miss the point," Rosalie said, ruffling my hair. "But that's understandable. Look, come to dinner next week. He's going out of town. We'll pick a night when my mother has a family circle meeting and we're free to talk. Sleep over."

Speaking of mothers, I wondered how and when Rosalie was going to tell hers this latest piece of news. But she said she had to run. She said he knew a little Italian place in the Village.

10

That night I dreamed it was 1933. Robert and I were having a big catered wedding in a hall, I in a slinky white satin gown and long veil, he in a rented tuxedo and a top hat that made his ears stick out and his nose look longer. He had taken off his glasses but he still had pimples. In the dream Robert kept smiling. I kept crying. It was like another awful dream I used to have when I was little about being dragged into a barbershop by my mother to have all my long hair cut off. When I woke up even the thought of seeing Robert again made me sick. I told myself that the actual haircut, which took place years later in a stylish beauty parlor, was very becoming and felt positively liberating. That Robert's nose wasn't that bad, that acne could be cured, that his contribution to the Haganah—but it was no use. Even my father had laughed at that one. Poor Robert. He would never know what hit him. Neither would my mother. Had she been at the wedding? I wasn't sure, though there was somebody holding up a sign that said CPA.

I forced myself to open my eyes, and for a moment imagined I was still dreaming. There was a shadowy figure sitting on the edge of my bed. But no, it was only my brother Walter, home on a delayed twenty-four-hour pass. How long had he been there? He didn't say. Only that he had been traveling all day and had to leave again in the morning, which was the kind of thing that happened to Walter—no Edleman princeling he. Then he just sat there in his infantry uniform for a while, like a visitor from a far-off place, the war, where it was all dark and shadowy. It was vaguely flattering to have him sit on the edge of my bed, but also disturbing, like the business with Robert, somehow wrong, unreal. . . . If I had had an older sister, would he have sat on the edge of her bed instead? Could I have told her of the strange dark discomfort of being with him? . . . But I didn't have a sister. I had Rosalie, and she was better than a sister. She was my friend. I drifted off to sleep again. Liberating was Rosalie's word. For herself.

Needless to say, my "friend" didn't bother to call me or show up in school that week, though Dr. Houghton repeated her name inquiringly and a bit apprehensively a few times, and even Dr. Curtis looked up dreamily from his recording of Schubert's *"divine"* Trio and gazed around as if something—he wasn't sure what —were missing. In fact, it was amazing how little had changed, in spite of all of us, including Leonora, going around saying, "Can you really believe it's January 6, *1947*?" Dr. Slavitt continued caustic, Dr. Lorillard conscientiously returned our term papers early, stopping me midway on an icy walk between the English Building and the cafeteria to ask me again if I would like to come to dinner one night, perhaps during the intersemester break. I hid the Lamb paper away from Gerald as I had hidden his postcard from Leonora. ("A+," she had written on it. "This is one of the finest papers I have ever received from any student anywhere I have ever taught." It was terrifying. Was the woman mad?) And, of course, Gerald kept refusing to tell me who he was in love with, either because he was being coy or truly didn't remember what I was talking about. Still, by then it was Friday—what did the rest matter?—and here we were at last on the E train, falling against each other every time it lurched to a stop. Paradise enough, really paradise, though Gerald's features, handsomer than ever, were cast in a strange bronze sunburn, and he was busy practicing his voice exercises. Not "tee-hee" this time, "hee-hee," a newcomer, which involved raising his upper lip way above his teeth and panting like an insanely merry asthmatic. Across the way, several passengers put down their newspapers and stared at him, then being New Yorkers, shrugged and picked them up again. It was all supposed to make his vocal cords or throat muscles or whatever go limp so that his tenor could come out unimpeded. Obviously the best thing that could ever happen to Gerald's tenor was for it to be impeded. Yet, embarrassing as it was at the moment, being so public, I admired his persistence. That anybody with such a terrible voice could believe he was going to be a great singer. There was something so touchingly *boylike* in his utter lack of self-consciousness, his absolute determination to do the impossible.

"Come on, Gerald," I had wheedled him one last time as our express train idled at Forest Hills waiting to pull out the moment the local came rattling in. "Who *is* it?"

"Who's what?" Gerald said, unpeeling one of the several Milky Ways he had bought for our journey. I could read nothing from his smile. Maybe he was just enjoying the candy.

Outside at Waverly Place it was unexpectedly night, and snowing. Great big white flakes settled and melted on our heavy coats and books. We walked on a coating of thin silent snow, leaving footprints, over to the Greenwich Settlement House where Gerald raced upstairs for his lesson, leaving me to fill up the hour as I pleased. I put my heavy pile of books on the damp bench next to his libretti and decided to take a walk. It was still wet, still dark, still snowing, and suddenly the streets seemed poetic, a dream of another postwar era, the nineteen twenties. I tried to imagine myself a bohemian living in one of these narrow brick houses. Edna St. Vincent Millay, burning her candle at both ends. Elinor Wylie. To lower the tone, as Dr. Slavitt would say, My Sister Eileen, drinking cheap wine with her lover in a dim little Italian restaurant with checkered tablecloths. "Flaming youth," "passion," "poverty," "garrets," swirled in my head, garnered from courses and daydreams and private reading. But there was no use pretending. I was no bohemian and I knew it. Even the part in the first act of *La Bohème* where they burned Rudolfo's manuscript to keep warm scared me to death. Gerald could never understand what was wrong. But then Gerald never understood why women minded being raped either. Oh, Gerald. I was back at the Settlement House. Outside the snow kept falling. Inside Gerald kept caterwauling. When he emerged I had made my peace with reality. He was again doing those insanely merry "hee-hee's." But the snow was falling thicker and whiter, and at my side Gerald was tall and cheerful. His voice teacher, a former famous opera singer, no longer famous or an opera singer, had seen much ground for optimism. Gerald, of course, would have seen much ground for optimism anyhow.

At Gerald's suggestion, we walked on to Bleecker, where behind the curtain of snow a row of small Italian stores stood still and brightly lit, like storefronts in a stage set. We stopped in a bakery with a nineteenth-century marble counter and bought some cannoli, which we ate continuing on down the street.

"I guess these will keep us until we get home," Gerald said.

Home? "You don't want to look at that room? I mean, just for fun?"

"Oh, I forgot," Gerald said. "Okay. But I promised Mommy I'd be back for dinner."

Mommy. He forgot. Never mind. But then why did my heart suddenly sing? Why was the memory of that marble bakery counter so beautiful? The taste of my cannoli better than any madeleine dipped in tea?

"He's queer as a nine-dollar bill, you know."

"Who?" I said, putting my arm cozily through Gerald's.

"Sherwin Schiff."

"Oh, him," I said, forgetting the matter immediately. Sometimes he popped up at the Settlement House, driving Gerald half crazy. Now Gerald's voice teacher talked of wanting Sherwin to do the choreography for a small production of the *Coffee Cantata*.

"It's just a set of unfortunate mannerisms," I said. "You really shouldn't think that just because . . ."

The address of Maria's find was attached to a small tiled building across the street from the Whitney. The Whitney was terra-cotta red and inside there was a painting of an old New York family with about twelve children grouped in a red Victorian living room. Across the street, Maria's green-tiled building opened into a small green-tiled hallway, with mailboxes and buzzers lining the wall. I started warily up the stairs with Gerald climbing behind me, a Gerald who every time I looked back oddly showed no fear or trepidation at all, the same Gerald who had talked about his Mommy and having to get home. On the third floor, I opened the door to Number 6 with Maria's second key, and Gerald walked past me and managed to turn on a swaying nautical lamp with a cheap blotched shade. I took one look and backed out again. I had never seen anything quite so ugly and small, what with that lamp and the narrow lumpy daybed and the raw little chest of drawers. The communal bathroom out in the hall was even worse, harsh and yellow under the naked bulb in the ceiling. "Douche," Rosalie had once said apropos of nothing. "Douche." I was very scared and I wanted to go home. What kind of loneliness would it be to live, really live in a furnished room like that?

When I went back in, Gerald had sat down on the daybed in his damp overcoat, seeming to occupy all of it.

"I like it," Gerald said.

"You like it?"

Gerald unloosed his tie and reached for the lamp.

"Gerald, what are you doing?" The lights went out. Could this possibly be the moment I had been waiting for almost my whole life? No. Oh no. I mean I wasn't even dressed for it. My hair was wet. I was wearing a stretched-out sleeveless red-and-white-striped boucle pullover. A blue skirt only 20 percent wool. My pink underwear was also rayon and left over from wartime. But Gerald was lost in a purpose of his own. He was pulling down my skirt, pulling that pullover over my head. All without passion, which was most surprising of all. We lay together naked on the narrow bed. I could feel from the movement of the mattress that Gerald was doing something to himself. Did boys do that openly, lying beside girls? It didn't bother me. I wasn't scared anymore, just quiet and alert, like before seeing the dentist. There was a thin squeaky rubber sound. I waited. "Gerald, what are you *doing?*" I whispered in the darkness, suddenly beside myself with excitement. He got on top of me and gently, gently, poked his way against a brick wall. I wasn't quite sure what was supposed to happen, but it didn't. He was hurting me, but it was a glorious hurt. "Never mind," Gerald said, and turned over and did something more to himself, and then with a shudder lay still. Oh, Gerald, ex-of-the-silly-sailor-suit! How close and adoring I felt. We got up and dressed quickly and separately. So many mysteries had been revealed, things I had wondered about for years. For example, how did you work up the nerve to take your clothes off? You didn't. *He* did it for you. I was ecstatic. Should I tell Rosalie? No, Rosalie had been to the Algonquin. It didn't matter. That nothing had actually happened seemed to make me even happier.

"We'll try again next *Saturday*," Gerald said.

12

The lobby of Rosalie's house was very large and exceedingly empty. A dark mahogany table stood alone in the center of the floor, and high up near the ceiling dim Spanish pillars supported a vacant balcony. The whole place was bathed in an eerie blue light. Gerald had once said interestedly that it was a perfect setting for the last act of *Don Giovanni.* I hurried across to the elevator, hearing the clatter of my high heels on the tiled floor, and took the shaky ride upstairs, glad when I got to Rosalie's floor of the sudden smell of cooking and of babies.

Mrs. Golden showed me in. I had never seen her look quite so Russian. It worried me for Rosalie's sake.

"Ah, my dear, I'm glad to see you," she said, gripping my hands in both her own. She kissed me on the cheek, and her face powder was musky, like her voice. It was her habit to dress up for Rosalie's friends, to make them feel more welcome, and tonight she was wearing a black satin dress that Rosalie often borrowed but couldn't always button, with a high regal collar that mounted in back and caught at a familiar pair of long rhinestone earrings. Her brown hair was crossed and braided at the top of her head like a coronet, and as usual she had touched up her cheekbones with rouge to make them look higher, more Slavic. But her eyes were red-rimmed, her smile a bit too bright, and I had a sinking feeling she had been crying.

"Rosalie is in the bedroom, tweezing her eyebrows," Mrs. Golden said, then led me into the living room where Rosalie's kid brother Clifton lolled on an armchair looking mixed up. He left the room when he saw me. I started to leave too and find Rosalie, but Mrs. Golden caught at my wrist.

"The room is lovely at this hour," she said tremulously, "don't you think?" It was six o'clock but I looked around anyway, following the line of her hand with its flashing rings past two overstuffed green brocaded chairs that matched the green brocaded sofa, a curved mahogany china closet filled with Grand Concourse teacups, the grand piano with Rosalie's high school graduation picture on top of it next to a fluted glass vase containing three real pink rosebuds.

"Yes, I know we don't have the best location in the world," Mrs. Golden said, staring at the piano with particular bitterness. "But can anyone say I haven't made the most of it? Not to be personal, you, my dear, may also realize that human beings can live in the Bronx as well as Manhattan—" She must have seen something on my face because she added, "but why should I chide you when my own daughter won't listen. Never mind. It doesn't matter. When I'm dead it definitely won't matter. If only somebody would kill me now, stab me and get it over with. . . . Forgive me, my dear, I'm just a foolish old lady mad with grief. Pay no attention. Enjoy life while you can." She lay back on the sofa, the hand that had gripped my wrist flung across her forehead.

I wondered whether she actually meant for me to leave her. It felt wrong, almost disloyal for me to be there alone with her when Rosalie was elsewhere. But she looked so young, so pretty, so vulnerable lying there, shimmering in her black satin, legs slightly bent. Pure St. Petersburg.

"If you only knew how alone I am in this world," she murmured, taking the words out of my mind. "No husband. A son who thinks it's beneath his dignity to deliver urine specimens part time. A daughter who, god knows why, hates me . . ."

She sat up, dabbing at her cheeks and smiling ruefully, more at herself than at me.

"I wonder—"

"Yes, Mrs. Golden?"

"I wonder—no, it's an unfair responsibility to put on someone so young."

"No, really."

"Well, I wonder if you could consider yourself *my* friend as well as Rosalie's. To give *me* advice. . . . Don't look so surprised. You have no idea how wise and mature you are for your age. How level-headed and dependable. I only wish Rosalie could be more like you, instead of only knowing how to get into trouble. But tell me—I beg of you—what do I do with her? I've tried everything, you know that. And now she's up to something again." She put up her hand to forestall me. "Please don't deny it. I can read all the signs. And if you only knew how grateful I am for this at least. That even if she won't confide in her own mother she still has you. Oh, my dear, if you only know how much Rosalie loves you. How she *trusts* you." She cradled my hand in both of hers. Her rings flashed gently in the light.

"So talk to her and tell me what she says."

"Oh, now wait a minute, Mrs. Golden, I can't—"

She put a finger over my lips, slipped a loose hairpin into her coronet braid, and went off to the kitchen. A few minutes later Rosalie and I heard her call out in a gay teary voice that dinner was ready.

It was very late when Rosalie and I finished talking and there was a weary solemn feeling in the air. I opened her bedroom window to get rid of some of the cigarette smoke. There were two creased hollows in the red chintz roses of her studio couch cover, and I shook it out and folded it over a chair. I had put off mentioning Gerald and now I didn't want to anymore. Rosalie came back from the bathroom in her nightgown. I had gone first.

"Listen, Rosie," I said, "I've been thinking. When the time comes, you can't just leave your mother a note. You have to discuss it."

"Oh, god," Rosalie said, "can't you see there are more important things to consider?"

"What things?" I said.

"Well, look at me. Just take a look at me."

"Oh, that. No girl looks good when she's going to bed."

"You don't understand," Rosalie said. She walked

over to the mirror and looked at herself dismally front and sideways, sucking in her stomach. It didn't help much. The stretchy pink jersey of her nightgown still clung to her hips and sagged around her breasts. "Come here," she said, beckoning to me with her finger. "Come here and tell me what you see."

"Us," I said, joining her reluctantly. It felt stupid standing there in my blue broadcloth pajamas.

"But this isn't *me*. Look at this. Is this me?"

"It's a few pimples."

"And there. Is that me?"

"You didn't wash off all your mascara and it smeared, that's all. Come to bed, Rosie."

"And here?"

"You need a brassiere."

"I need one desperately. And what about these big fat hips? And this hair that looks like a bush? Why deceive ourselves? I'm fat and horrible. I look like a woman of forty. I'm a mess."

We turned away and sat down on her bed, watching Rosalie's chipped and painted toenails toy forlornly with her unraveled hem. "No, there's no use," Rosalie said. "I was looking at myself in the bathroom before and I had a real moment of truth. I mean, suppose he catches me like this and thinks it's the real me? What will he say? I'm scared. I feel sick."

"But he saw you in the hotel."

"The lights were out."

"Let's go to sleep," I said.

"Maybe I could get up very early and put on a girdle and makeup before he's awake," Rosalie said. "And at night I could leave it all on. Or else, I was looking at some nightgowns today, and I saw a black satin one with red ribbons and these sequins. So, maybe—"

It was really very late. Rosalie, I thought, Rosalie darling, please give up on those sequins. But Rosalie without her sequins would be Rosalie in that sleazy pink nightgown and she was right—that wasn't Rosalie.

"You're just emotionally exhausted," I said.

"Hm?"

I kissed her on the forehead. She was sweating. We lay in the dark thinking together.

13

As arranged, Gerald stood waiting for me under the marquee of the Waverly Theater, tall, handsome, still a bit sunburned, looking for me in the wrong direction, and, not at all to my surprise, a complete stranger. I wanted to get it over with. Why had I gotten all dressed up in my Persian-lamb coat, and hand-painted blouse, and cocktail ring? Practically the same outfit I wore to the library? Why had I bought that black lacy underwear that didn't make me look sexy but under-nourished and in mourning? I made myself walk faster. Of course, he was dressed up too, in a belted gabardine coat and brown felt hat. Maybe he should have sent me an orchid. Maybe if we had both come staggering out of the subway as we used to, disheveled and loaded down with books and briefcases. Maybe if he hadn't come on time and I had had to stand there waiting for *him*. No, no maybes. I was already at his elbow. "Gerald?" I said, amazed that my voice carried. He turned around with a startled look, then smiled and bent to kiss me on the cheek.

"Gerald," I said, kissing him back, "there's something I must tell you—"

What it was, Gerald wasn't waiting to hear. He had taken my hand and was leading me like a child across the busy traffic of Sixth Avenue. I looked back yearningly at the movie marquee: *Nobody Lives Forever*, with John Garfield.

"Gerald—"

"Wait here," Gerald said, depositing me outside of Whelan's.

"What do you need in a drugstore?" I said anxiously.

"Cough drops."

"No, really."

In a few minutes he came out again, and once more, taking me by the hand like an idiot child, led me down Eighth Street to the dark green-tiled building that was the opposite of the beautiful red Whitney across the way. Upstairs, with one of the keys I had handed over to him, he unlocked the door of Number 6 and switched on the nautical lamp. It was even uglier, smaller, more squalid than I had remembered. Gerald, curiously domestic, located a closet and hung our coats on wire hangers. His hat he put on the shelf.

"Gerald, listen," I blurted out, "I changed my mind."

"I knew you'd say that," Gerald said unperturbed, pulling down the spread, putting a little brown paper bag on the night table.

"No, really, I mean it. I'm not kidding. I've been giving the matter a great deal of thought and the only reason I didn't bring it up in school was that it obviously wasn't appropriate. But don't you see, the reason nothing happened last time was that nothing was supposed to happen. We have to read the signs. Gerald, we're *friends*. Platonic friends. Don't you want to stay platonic friends?"

Gerald took a little jar of vaseline out of the paper bag.

"How does that blouse of yours come off?" he said, putting out the light again.

Afterwards, I adored him. He gave me a kiss, a little husbandly kiss at the end. "You don't do that for everybody," Gerald said, and dozed off. How could he be so sleepy when I was wide awake and literally aching with tenderness? The vaseline had done the trick. I had thought that penetration, a cojoining was enough. But there was more. Gerald, during: "How are you?" Me: "Fine, thanks, how are you?" Gerald: "Oh, god." But he had kissed me anyhow, and when he went to sleep didn't turn away. He woke up, and we made love again. I was getting the hang of it. When we put on the lights finally, I saw to my amazement that the sheet was streaked with brownish blood. It was as wonderful as it was astonishing. How proud I was of that blood. How proud I was of my charley horse for days afterward. No one had ever told me it involved musculature. It made me feel so close to him, to everyone. Seated on the wicker bench of the E train I wanted everybody to know why I winced each time I bounced, why, sliding into my seat in classes, I lowered myself so gingerly. I thought of poor Gerald yawning, and laughed and laughed. But how could he have been so sleepy when I was so alive?

Two

The letter from the Joint Distribution Committee that my DP cousin was finally coming over coincided with a very curious phenomenon. I had begun to worry terribly that Gerald wasn't Jewish. Not for my own sake but my father's. Every time I looked at my father I felt sick with guilt. There was a seamed sunburned quality to the back of his neck that was especially heartbreaking. I didn't know why. I kissed him on the back of his neck many times, to his surprise and mine. I hadn't done that since I was about twelve. The irony was that Gerald "passed" so easily. He looked Jewish enough, he acted Jewish enough, he even signed himself L. Gerald Muster, which was ridiculous, since only Jews ever did that, used a blind first initial to cover up names like Irving. In Gerald's case it was for Laurence, "Mommy's" family name. Also "Mommy," in spite of being an Episcopalian, wore the same upswept hairdo, ankle-strap shoes, and silver fox jacket as Mrs. Edleman. Maybe it was just an all-purpose bitch-mother costume. Only Gerald's height revealed that he wasn't of immigrant stock, but Martin Edleman was almost as tall. The other joke, if you wanted to call it that, was that my parents liked Gerald fine, not even minding if he called as late as one in the morning, my mother of course listening in avidly on the extension. No doubt, in her heart, and practical considerations aside, she much preferred him to Robert. He was handsomer and he ate more, which he did at my house very frequently, at mealtimes and in between. Another fly in the ointment. We no longer had a place of our own to go to.

"How *dare* you?" Maria had said furiously, catching me by the elbow in the cafeteria. "How *dare* you?"

"How dare I what?" I said, feeling my heart pound terribly, holding on to my tray to keep things from sloshing over. I had been hurrying back to where Gerald had risen and kissed me on the cheek. Gerald always stood up now and kissed me when I came into the cafeteria.

"Using our room for that!"

What did she think I was going to use it for? "I don't believe I have to dignify that with an answer," I said.

"And those filthy sheets bundled into a corner of the closet."

She had me there. I should have sent them to the laundry, replaced them, anything. I had been so fastidious as a child, a doctor had once told my parents to *make* me get dirt on my pants. But I couldn't bear to throw those sheets away, certainly not wash the lovely bloodstains out. Lady Macbeth in reverse. Dr. Houghton would have appreciated that.

"I'll give you back your keys. You may keep the entire rest of the month's rent," I said, trying for some more dignity. "Forgive me for offending your sensibilities."

"Oh, Lois," Maria said, letting go, sighing with exquisite sensitivity. "You must try to appreciate my view of the matter. I happen to have a very low pain threshold. I can't tolerate ugliness. I hate ugliness."

Later, too late, in the middle of the night in fact, I thought no, she loves it because she sees it everywhere. When her silly mother told her to turn down a recording of the *Wintereise*, when Betty Rubin, about to be engaged as usual, told us about a recipe in the *Ladies' Home Journal* that began with raw fish fillets and Maria stopped her with a hand upraised, eyes shut. But at that moment, feeling sick, besmirched, I just went on to our regular table where Robby Wilson was helping red-headed Luke Lazar, still our potential song-and-dance man, with his elementary calculus, while Gerald was telling Sherwin Schiff about Maggie Teyte's fantastic affair with Sir Thomas Beecham. "Not *really!*" Sherwin said. "Absolutely. 'Of them all,' she said, 'Sir Thomas Beecham was the best.'" As I listened, soothed and somehow sweetened, I suddenly wondered if I had *wanted* Maria to find those sheets. In just that condition. A terrible thought, which I would never ever confide to anyone. Never mind. I had known from the beginning that I wasn't cut out for *la vie bohème*, maybe even Greenwich Village altogether. True, it left me and Gerald high and dry, but we would manage. There was his father's car—Mr. Muster was a traveling salesman—my father's car—not that I thought I could actually do it in that Buick—the fact that his parents went to Miami, mine to Lakewood. How unfair, though, that Maria should be so popular with the boys, have a million dates, even more than Betty

Rubin, boys who never dreamed how much she loathed them. Poor stupid fools. I looked at my beautiful Gerald, now finishing up my potato chips, with something more than love, a feeling almost familial. Yes, we would manage. It might even be better, more respectable.

2

Still, waiting on the DP pier with my parents that afternoon at the end of January, I deliberately banished Gerald from my mind. Also Rosalie, also Luke Lazar and his dreams of writing a great musical comedy for her, also Leonora and her subscription to *Partisan Review*, everything, as if I were a nun keeping myself pure on that rough wooden wharf washed in its cold underwater blue light. In fact, it literally was cold and we had been waiting for hours, my mother in her black Persian-lamb coat and fat little crisscross sandals, complaining interminably about the drafts and that her feet hurt, my father teasing her indulgently about being dressed so fancy though it was he who had decked her out like a Christmas tree, a metaphor he would hardly have appreciated, but I was sore. I was sore about everything, especially the talk around me. "I hear the ones from the concentration camps are the worst. Animals." "That's what you had to be to survive." Another fact was that the ship had docked long ago and people had been coming off it for ages, but the droning of names through a microphone had also long ago droned us out of expectancy. They all came off wearing tags, like war orphans, clothes on a discard pile. I looked at a tagged woman standing nearby, waiting patiently to be claimed. She was holding a child, a boy of about two with sprawling limbs as if he had grown large in her arms. He was crying, but beyond holding him the woman did nothing. She was wearing a brown coat, a red felt hat with a veil. Her short lank hair was held back behind her ears with two bobby pins. Of it all the veil was somehow the worst. Then, finally, we heard, *"Josef Ackerman, Ackerman, Ackerman . . . ,"* in fact my father heard it first, and there he was, exactly like that passport picture, except maybe more intriguing because of his trench coat and a fedora with a sloping brim. My father, Manny Ackerman to the hilt, busied himself with small arrangements, after we had all kissed each other stiffly and self-consciously. And through it all, Josef kept smiling, an unnervingly humble smile, as if he thought he would give us less trouble if he *looked* happy. All the way home in the taxi, he never stopped smiling, hardly even glancing out of the window, though we were endlessly pointing out sights and places, and only looked down for a moment surprised, even a bit frightened, when I suddenly tore off his tag and threw it crumpled onto the floor. I was still thinking about that veil. In the self-service elevator he kept tight hold of his small cardboard suitcase, relinquishing it finally on the studio couch in Walter's room, where it looked as lonely and deserted as the furniture. My father showed him where and how to wash up, and we all sat down to dinner in the foyer, talking a peculiar and broken blend of Yiddish and English, Josef's English better than I would have expected, my parents' Yiddish curiously and suddenly inadequate. They had put a big white napkin in his lap, pointed to forks and spoons, and finally after a few questions about relatives—all missing, dead—sat there discussing him openly, wondering if he were religious, if he had deliberately put those finger waves in his hair. The maid took him in her stride, up to and including the baked apples. He was clearly not the one to please.

"So how do you like the way we live in this country, Yosel?" my father said, assuming automatically that my cousin would follow when he got up and headed for the living room. "Wall-to-wall carpeting."

"*Schoen.*"

"Video."

"*Schoen.*"

"Daddy, for godssakes, stop showing off to him."

My mother looked from one to the other of us, worried.

"No, she's absolutely right, Celia," my father said, settling down before his beloved set. "Whatever we have, it's certainly better than what he's used to."

I took Josef by the hand and led him back into Walter's room to unpack his suitcase. It took almost no time at all. Everything he owned fit into Walter's bottom bureau drawer. What was left were a few things wrapped in tissue paper, which, still smiling, he brought back into the living room. Presents. An Italian mosaic cigarette box for my father, who curtly said thank you and put it next to his humidor, a beautiful enormous linen tablecloth for my mother, with gray hand-embroidered fretwork on its corners. "You don't have to waste your money on those things," my father said. "No, no, Manny," my mother said, feeling the cloth between a practiced thumb and forefinger, seeing it very clearly as imported. "Why shouldn't he if it's his pleasure?"

I unwrapped my own small present from its pink tissue paper. We all looked at each other. It was a small gold wristwatch.

"Give it back," my father said. Then to Josef, "No, I'm sorry. In this country we don't give watches to strange girls."

"I'm not a strange girl," I said. "I'm his cousin."

"Look, Yosel," my father said, "you have to understand that in this country when you give a girl a watch it means—"

"It doesn't mean anything," I said. "He doesn't understand what it means. It's a present. I'm keeping it."

"You're giving him ideas, Lois. I'm warning you."

"I'm keeping it."

My father turned back to his television, and my mother wandered off to the kitchen to worry the maid, who was still cleaning up. I pulled a hassock over to the sofa, where Josef was sitting stiffly by himself in the middle, hardly making a dent in the cushions. It was painful to look at him. Not only because of those expressionless hazel eyes, the meager flesh of his face, his suit so ill-matched and worn—brown jacket, blue pencil-striped trousers. No, it was the eager *docility* of him, gentility almost, the neat ridges into which his hair was combed—his "finger waves" as they had called them—the carefully mended collar of his clean shirt. He pointed to his presents on the coffee table.

"You like?"

"Oh, yes, very much."

"In the camp," he said, in a mixture of Yiddish and English, "they would give us passes. We would walk in the streets and look in the stores. It's a beautiful world, we would say, but not for us."

"Daddy, tell him he doesn't have to cry anymore."

"You have a tongue."

But Josef was smiling again, and after looking at my father to see if it was okay to watch television with him, finally picked up a copy of *Life*, which lay among his presents on the coffee table, and began to leaf through it. Something on the back cover caught his attention and he stared at it until my mother offered him a glass of tea, which he politely refused.

"It's late," my father said. "Come on, Yosel. Let's get to bed. You too, Lois."

Josef obediently followed him, but I stayed behind, longing to make my usual phone calls, but somehow sticking to my vow—of what? Chastity? Self-abnegation? Instead I picked up the copy of *Life* and wondered what had interested Josef so on the back cover. But it was only a ridiculously romantic perfume ad, with an elegantly dressed couple in evening clothes embracing on a balcony. I looked at the front cover, which featured a photo essay on the Renaissance Man, then started to leaf through the rest: trouble in Palestine, another photo essay on the much maligned profession of psychoanalysis—and looked up to find that Josef had returned. He was dressed in a neat pair of printed blue pajamas, and was wearing a hairnet tied in the back. I had never seen a man in a hairnet before.

"What do they do in this picture?" Josef asked, sitting next to me on the couch, and flipping the copy of *Life* over again to its back cover. Besides the hairnet, he also smelled strongly of brilliantine.

"It's an ad," I said. "An advertisement. They're trying to sell some silly perfume. America's like that. Hideously commercial."

Josef shook his head and smiled, a very different smile this time, with a glint of gold in the back. "What do the man and woman do?"

"They're kissing each other."

"And what is kissing?"

"Oh, Josef, *you* know. It's—"

"Is kissing like this?"

Oh, god. I had drawn away so quickly, I was ashamed. Smiling *my* awful smile, I offered him my cheek. He caught me full on the lips.

"Well, good night, Josef," I said, getting up as fast as I decently could, and remembering to take along the wristwatch. "Oh, yes, and thank you for the present. . . . And, oh, yes, welcome."

"No, no good night. No welcome."

But I had already hurried to the safety of my room and closed the door. I caught myself wiping my mouth.

Maybe I should tell him about Gerald, pretend I was officially engaged? No! I refused. I put the gold wristwatch on my bureau, trying not to think of how carefully it had been wrapped in pink tissue paper in a DP camp in Bari.

3

He was always there, clean, upright, expectant, wearing a new maroon sweater, sitting in the armchair in Walter's room with a magazine in his hands, which he immediately put down as soon as he saw me pass down the hall. Then he would come into my room and sit in my armchair, asking first if it was all right. Yes, it was fine, I would say, doing my homework with the full weight of his presence behind me. Not that he was going to stay there forever. My father, having outfitted him fresh from head to toe, was looking for a job for him. It was not so easy. He was an upholsterer by trade and there were union problems, problems which Josef, perfectly willing to be a scab, did not either understand or appreciate. The general plan was that once work was found he would move to a furnished room, maybe in Brooklyn where he had relatives on his mother's side. Meanwhile, though eager to work, he seemed in no hurry to move. I think he thought we were either rich or crazy or both. He didn't like his new clothes. His shoes, in particular, he felt were not expensive enough. He thought you could walk to Brooklyn and laughed when we said you couldn't. "I don't like the *smell* of that guy," my father said repeatedly. "Who the hell even knows if he belongs to us?" "Oh, Daddy, for godssake, the resemblance alone—" But it was my father who nonetheless bought the two suits, extra shirts, new sweaters, insufficiently expensive shoes, called prospective employers; my mother who, with the maid, supplied him with food, took care of his laundry. While I, his great champion in the abstract, did absolutely nothing except feel guilty, and wish in my heart that the family resemblance were *not* so plain, that he truly was an adventurer, a piece of wreckage cast up from the sea, battening on our generosity until he drifted on to other shores. The plain truth, metaphors aside, was that he simply scared me to death. I wasn't sure why. Night after night he told us stories, some of them hard to believe, which I listened to, especially the hardest to believe, with the same reverential attention I did the oratorios I went to with Gerald in different churches around the city. Fleeing from the Russians, Josef said, he had been captured by the Germans. They had loved him, he boasted, treated him as a pet, never found out he was Jewish. ("What's the matter? They never caught him with his pants down?" my father said. *Daddy!* I cried, helplessly half thinking of Gerald, but then the lights were always out and would I know the difference?) Or, it could be something as simple as:

"Once I went back to Brest-Litovsk. Find the house? I couldn't even find the street."

4

"I guess it's just that he's always *there*," I said to my friends in the cafeteria, most of whom wanted to see him.

"What about the English lessons?" Leonora said, laughing predictably, going straight for the jugular, as usual. "The little cultural expeditions?"

"You could take him to a museum," Milton Schwartz said. "It would transcend any language problems."

He was being sweet and I ought to have been more grateful. Actually, Milton and Gerald and I were very often now a threesome. It was nice having him around. He was gifted, he was serious, he was modest, of everyone the most likely to realize his ambition of being an artist. Also devoted, almost doglike in his fidelity and application to his work and his friends, slightly dog-eared in appearance. In addition, he accepted the fact of being poor. Often Gerald and I visited him in the Bronx, on the other side of the Concourse from Rosalie, and it never occurred to him that it wasn't good enough for him. His mother, a widow like Mrs. Golden, was a very nice old-fashioned lady, who entertained us amid antimacassars and bowls of fruits and nuts with nutcrackers sticking into them. His older sister Myrna, a schoolteacher, was already patently an old maid. But Milton protected her as he would have protected me or Gerald if we were exposed or in trouble. He took

Myrna to our parties, and when he decided as a result of Gerald's misguided advice to take voice lessons, Myrna took voice lessons too. I had a feeling sometimes that Milton's dying father had years ago told Milton to mind poor Myrna—we called her "poor Myrna" in one phrase—and Milton was still minding her. It would have been the same if you had told Milton to hold up a painting while you found a picture hook or something. Three weeks later, he would still be there, one hand against the wall, picture hook notwithstanding. It was Leonora, of course, who pointed out that Milton looked as if he didn't wash much, and of course it was true. He was handsome but sort of seedy. You had to go over him feature by feature to see how good-looking he actually was. Get past the collars turning up at the edges, the hands stained with paints and ink. His complexion, merely olive, looked swarthy, his beautiful black wavy hair started too low on his forehead, so that it seemed to meet his heavy black eyebrows. He was tall, not as tall as Gerald, but a good six feet. Only, his broad shoulders and long arms made him look squat. Still, he was absolutely the best friend in the world. I loved walking across campus between him and Gerald, feeling like Ginger Rogers, except that we were talking about politics, life, the role of the artist, what would happen to Rosie the Riveter now that the boys were home, whether Henry Moore was a genius or a fraud, opera in English, how to impeach Truman. He was absolutely loyal to Gerald and me. Also to Rosalie, who when she made an appearance he would often engage in long serious conversations in her secluded corner of

the cafeteria. Once I told him what it was like sometimes to arrive at Medaglia early in the morning, and he
understood that too. I would leave my house in boots,
heavy winter coat, muffler wound around my head, de-
scend to the E train right in the middle of Manhattan,
though dressed for an expedition to the Antarctic.
Then, forty-five minutes later, after maybe a quick bout
with *Troilus and Cressida*, a rushing glance at 67th
Avenue to see if Gerald were waiting and I should get
out and join him at the express stop, most of the time
not, I would emerge at Jamaica, wait on line for the bus
to Flushing. It was snowy country. We passed a
snowed-in country club, the agricultural high school
next door where, if it were early enough, cocks were
still crowing. I would get out, trudge up the slick icy
hill past the combination Administration Building and
auditorium, adobe with a red tiled roof, and then, right
in front of me, though at a great distance, was—Manhattan. Silver spires shimmering on a silver platter.
Manhattan. Had I traveled so far to see something so
near? Milton understood this.

5

It was hard to say which was more shocking, Leonora's
engagement, or her way of announcing it. She simply
showed up at the cafeteria one day with a diamond engagement ring. The point was that even if Leonora was

engaged, astounding enough, what was she doing with a *ring?* That was for sorority girls, for Betty Rubin, for imbeciles who used Pond's. Yet, there it was, a diamond of modest size, glimmering on a pink finger. Leonora smiled when we noticed it and offered very little information. No, it wasn't Jeff. His name was Herman (!) and he was a graduate of the Wharton School of Business (!). Since she added nothing more, there were soon all kinds of rumors afloat. That Herman was working as an accountant for her father, the furrier. That she was pregnant and needed to get married in a hurry. That her brother, Martin, was the one who had made her pregnant. (This last from Sherwin Schiff.) Only Maria Gato remained apart from all our excited titillation and curiosity. Heart-faced and intent, she listened darkly to Leonora's amusing anecdotes while the rest of us laughed, watched the little diamond ring flash in the light when Leonora made one of her grand gestures, followed her with her prune eyes when Leonora gathered up her coat, books, the latest issue of *Partisan Review* and left the cafeteria.

"She won't go through with it, you know," Maria said one day when we were alone at the littered table.

"What do you mean, won't go through with it?"

Maria shrugged. "Because the marks are on her."

"What marks? I don't know what you're talking about."

Maria gave me a half-mocking smile, and turned away again.

"She told me so herself one night," Maria said. "She

said, 'The marks have been on me since I was thirteen years old.'"

"Oh, shut up," I said, gathering my stuff together. I waited for her to tell me not to be cruel. But instead she just sat there alone in her leather jacket, still smiling, that terrible smile, which was so much more like a Greek mask of tragedy than of comedy.

Luckily, Gerald was already waiting for me at the bottom of the hill, among the first on line at the bus stop. Had he got there early or elbowed his way up front? It was Friday, music-lesson day, and we were going to make a detour at his apartment to pick up some extra music. His teacher had changed her mind about the *Coffee Cantata* and they were now tentatively planning a chamber version of *The Marriage of Figaro*, in English, with Gerald as musical director, and Sherwin Schiff as choreographer and principal Spanish dancer. For practice, Sherwin pranced around in black tights and a red snood. "Queer as a nine-dollar bill," Gerald said. "Oh, Gerald," I said, laughing helplessly, wishing that he would let up on the subject for a change, wishing that Maria had not said that terrible thing about Leonora and her marks. *Oiseau de malheur*, I thought, remembering my French, *oiseau de malheur*. Why didn't she get lost? And yet, the fact was that without Maria and that little room we shared the rent for on Eighth Street, my excursions to the Village with Gerald were no longer quite so thrilling, so full of shivery anticipation. We wandered around, bought our cannoli at the marble-topped counter of the Italian bakery on Bleecker, sometimes had our dinner at the

White Tower Hamburger Shop on Sixth Avenue before we went our separate ways. My mother was puzzled and complaining. What was the use of a maid, she said, who was only for me in the first place? That Friday Gerald's apartment happened to be empty. His mother was in the hospital with some female complaint, his father on the road. There was a dinette and a dropped living room, both very clean and shadowy. Gerald's room was also strikingly dark and unoccupied. I looked at his bed with the plaid boy's-room spread. "Come on," Gerald said, pulling me by the arm. "But, Gerald—" "Not in my room," Gerald said. "Not while Mommy's away."

6

We did many, many other things while Mommy was away, however, some of them okay, some of them better not to think about later. Milton Schwartz was hardly ever involved in the better-not-to-think-about-later episodes. He had no money to fool around with, for one thing. Once, at Joey's roadside tavern, when I was treating to French fries to go with our beers he even asked could he have a hamburger instead, since it came to the same thing, ten cents. Or, offered a cigarette, he would take it and put it into a little tin box reserved for the purpose, including butts he had snuffed out and was also saving. I sometimes saw Dr. Lorillard watching us over her cocktail, as from a great distance. For another thing, Milton had somewhere along the line acquired a girlfriend, a nice big blowsy blonde named Ruthie, a far cry altogether from his usual crushes on types like Betty Rubin, who not only avoided him like the plague and went around in bobby sox but now boasted of wearing *Junior* Tampax. Ruthie went to Pratt and consequently while we saw less of Milton we kidded him more. "Did you ever do it standing up?" Sherwin Schiff asked. "Sure, it's nice. It makes you feel more like a human being. . . ." Evidently they had been standing up a great deal because the next thing we knew we had all received engraved invitations to Milton's wedding at a big reform temple in Forest Hills, near where Ruthie lived in a one-family house with a Ping-Pong table in the basement. The invitations shook us up. What was this, an epidemic? Leonora's diamond engagement ring. Now Milton's engraved invitations. ("Not engraved," Leonora said, smiling, running her forefinger, not her engagement finger, over it: "Raised.") Our social activities increased, partly no doubt as a result of our uneasiness. We went to the ballet at the City Center. We went tea-dancing at the Plaza, Rosalie, Luke Lazar, Gerald and I, emerging so drunk that Rosalie in her high-heeled ankle-straps walked down Fifth Avenue on her ankles. We subscribed to the Museum of Modern Art, Gerald and I as a married couple, in order to split the cost of the subscription, which had now gone up to $12.50, and also lunch in the grown-up splendor of the members' room. "Mr. and Mrs. Gerald Muster," the card said, which considering the present atmosphere, was creepy.

Nevertheless, the day of Milton's wedding arrived, and there we sat as in the cafeteria, but all lined up, and in a terrible state of nervous confusion. The place was like the Roxy (*"B'Nai* Roxy," Leonora said), huge, with red velvet seats, and a raised altar backed with a wrought-gold breastplate that looked as if it had been lifted from some gigantic Byzantine whore. "Poor Myrna" was a skinny maid of honor, there were relatives on each side. Against this glittering architectural monstrosity, this profusion of uncles and aunts, pale blue dresses, corsets, rented tuxedos, sweet-pea corsages, Milton and Ruthie were diminished and small. Also calm. Worse than calm. Before the ceremony I had caught sight of Ruthie laughing under her white veil. I had never seen a laughing bride before. I thought of my nightmare about Robert. Why weren't they railing against fate? Getting married was almost obscene. Having a baby was truly disgusting. After a catered reception in the basement where the reform rabbi, *sans yarmulke,* shook our hands and asked us unctuous questions, Gerald and Rosalie and I quickly took the subway to the Russian Tearoom, to meet her boyfriend, who was still in a state of marital limbo. We got even drunker than we had at the Plaza. Rosalie's boyfriend led us to the Algonquin where we let him do the registering because he was the oldest and at least seemed the most sober. Laughing uproariously, Gerald and I followed them up in the next elevator. Still laughing, we drank some more from Rosalie's boyfriend's flask, and then he put out the light. There were twin beds. We undressed, scrabbling, hilarious, in the darkness. Against the light from the airshaft, I could see that Sam was still wearing his hat, which made it all funnier still. Then I unexpectedly turned sober. "No, please, Gerald. Stop!" "Why?" "I've had enough." "Enough?" Gerald said, truly puzzled. "What's it like to have enough?" From the next bed Rosalie's boyfriend burst into wild hoots of laughter.

7

Josef, of course, had no idea why I suddenly decided to bring him to school the next day, any more than I did, except that it was the last week before the inter-semester break and I had promised. And of course nobody knew quite what to do with him, except be terribly polite. Robby Wilson politely inquired if he had thought about night school, Milton politely inquired whether he had seen the Henry Moore Show, Leonora politely inquired about the long pinky nail on his left hand, as long as Fu Manchu's, which Josef had explained to me a long time ago, and now almost condescendingly explained to my friends—night school and museums were also kind of beneath him—happened to be a fingernail essential for small mechanical tasks, such as slitting things open, or folding them down. I think he was surprised that we didn't all have them.

But then he was full of stuff like that, little unshakable convictions, that if you put ashes in somebody's drink when they weren't looking, they would get dead drunk, etc. The only curious exception in terms of comprehension was Dr. Slavitt, who, though he had taken his doctorate at Harvard, turned out to have been a City College undergraduate, and whose Yiddish was excellent. Speaking to Josef after class, an exegesis of the *Areopagitica*, he looked at me, naturally, with more contempt than ever, though his expression seemed to change when they got to talking politics, something about the Nazi-Soviet Pact, which I couldn't quite follow but on which they differed. Dr. Lorillard, who was polite to begin with, greeted him kindly, and then made a definite date with me to come to dinner the following week. I took Josef back home, depositing him with my parents, and got dressed to go out again. Luke Lazar, having wisely decided to leave school altogether, unlike Rosalie, who was still hanging in there by a thread, had wangled a job in the chorus of *Annie Get Your Gun*. My father, naturally, had come up with house seats, and Gerald had decided that in honor of the occasion, though he didn't like Luke, we should go formal. Maybe it was his way of upstaging him. I wore a beautiful lavender organza dress, courtesy of one of my father's associates in formal wear, with a lavender satin belt and lavender satin shoes to match. My Persian-lamb coat was slung over my shoulders. Gerald called for me, tall and stunning in his tuxedo. My DP cousin turned around from looking at the Golden Gloves on television to watch us leave. I showed him my wristwatch. I didn't much like the show, though it was exciting to see Luke, one of *us*, singing and dancing in cowboy clothes on an actual stage, and loved standing around the crowded lobby during intermission being part of a handsome young couple, though a bit mismatched in height. Poor Gerald had never danced cheek to cheek with a girl in his life, and I lived in dread that maybe one day he would. Afterwards, we waited at the stage door of the Imperial Theater until Luke emerged in full makeup, greeting people who didn't know him, and then went over to the Waldorf-Astoria where we sat in the Peacock Alley, drinking and laughing and toasting Luke's "triumph" and shaking our heads and laughing some more as Gerald pointed out all the fags in the cast. Gerald and I kissed and kissed in the automatic elevator when he brought me home ("No, don't kiss me back," Gerald said), and I drifted off to bed, full of the evening, the loveliest of ladies, letting my organza gown, my satin slippers, long white gloves, fall where they would, on the chair, on the floor, everywhere, like Scarlett O'Hara home from the ball. Oh, it was lovely.

The sense of a shadowy presence inside my doorway startled me awake. Then I relaxed again. Of course. It was only Walter. Dear silly Walter, home on one of his passes. I dreamily moved my feet to make room for him and half closed my eyes.

"Walter . . . ?"

Silence.

"Walter?"

"*Du schlafts?*" a voice whispered in an easy oily Yiddish.

I could make out the silhouette better now. An approaching male figure in pajamas and a dangling hairnet. He came still closer, reeking of brilliantine.

"What do you want?"

Josef laughed. "You're not afraid to sleep alone?"

"No."

"You're not afraid I'll come in during the night and try to do something?"

"No."

"Then maybe *I'm* afraid?"

"Josef, please go away. This isn't funny."

But he only laughed some more, looking around at my clothes strewn all over the place, then thrust his hand under my blanket. Oh, my god. I thought of Rosalie. I thought of yielding for moral reasons and killing myself afterwards. Then, *"Daddy!"* I cried, though my father couldn't hear me. And though he also knew my father couldn't hear me, Josef hesitated just a moment before he turned and went away. The next morning, sick with guilt, I told my father. By afternoon Josef had gone to live in a furnished room in Brooklyn.

8

"Stop aggravating yourself," my father said. "What are you aggravating yourself?" No, he just didn't understand. "I understand better than you think," my father said grimly, reaching into the jacket which was slung over the back of his chair. "Here. Take a cab. Buy the lady a box of candy. Enjoy yourself." "Live vile you young," my mother agreed, looking up from her fillet of sole and missing the point, as usual. "Celia—" I left them eating their dinner. There was no point in pursuing it. How could they understand, when all I could do was keep seeing Josef as he watched the Golden Gloves fights on television, and know in my heart that I had betrayed my deepest principles? I was glad Leonora wasn't around to laugh at me, another terrible sign of weakness. I bought flowers instead of candy, still feeling that I was about to visit my Aunt Rose and then, what the hell, took a cab.

Dr. Lorillard's maid took my flowers, a bunch of wintry yellow pompons, then waited for me to decide whether or not to fix my hair before she announced that "Mrs. Baldwin" was expecting me. Mrs. Baldwin/Dr. Lorillard. I was impressed in spite of myself, though Dr. Lorillard had warned me. Nevertheless, I wished whoever she was had not made such a point of inviting me. I wasn't in the mood, and already it was so different atmospherically from watching her powder her nose before her honors seminar. The idea of being someone who specialized in the Renaissance, or anything else for that matter, was utterly beyond me. Going to school might be the only thing I was good at, but I could less and less see myself as a scholar. It was all so musty and dreary, so selflessly devoted to the young when all I wanted to do now was grow up. Not that this elegant little apartment in the East Fifties was dreary, far from it. Even the elevator man was dressed in practically the same costume Gerald's music teacher had rented for the lackey in *The Marriage of Figaro,* complete with beige striped weskit and dickey. Had I been gauche to bring even flowers? Would I ever see my pompons again? I followed the maid into a small well-appointed living room where Dr. Lorillard, who had been sitting on a settee sipping a cocktail and leafing through a book, rose to greet me. Well-appointed. The phrase not only came to mind, but stayed there, though there was even more stuff than at Rosalie's, including things that didn't match, such as the different flowered chintzes on the sofa and chairs, and what appeared to be worm holes in some of the older tables. But all of it looked valuable and real, the blue and white china jars with little lids on them, a silver epergne—another impressive word—with salted almonds on one tier and flat white dinner mints on another, the small fireplace with genuine logs burning between two brass andirons. Only the picture above the mantelpiece set a false note, a turn-of-the-century lady dressed in pale blue, blue taffeta gown, blue bonnet tied with ribbons under her chin. The brushstrokes were visible, but it was too hackneyed and familiar, like a framed reproduction.

"Ah, so you like her work too?" Dr. Lorillard said, mistaking the nature of my gaze.

"I beg your pardon?"

"Mary Cassatt."

"Oh, yes," I said to be agreeable, though I had never heard of her.

"My aunt left it to me."

"How nice of her," I said, though actually I had

never heard of anyone who inherited anything either, except maybe life insurance, which didn't exactly come under the same heading. Dr. Lorillard, with one of her blurted laughs, asked me what I would like to drink. I turned away from the picture. "Whatever you're having."

"A martini? Good."

"Yes, a martini would be lovely," I said, following her into the kitchen and hovering around to watch her make it, rather as I did Mrs. Golden when she was preparing dinner. It was a tiny kitchen and she seemed surprised to find me behind her, though she immediately barked out another laugh and said, "John's specifications. I hope they're all right with you?" "Oh, fine." Since I had never had a martini before—it was definitely an evening of famous firsts—and it had taken a moment to realize that John was her husband—everybody else I knew, including Milton's wife Ruthie, called their husbands "my husband"—I watched the process, ritual rather, with great interest, feeling somehow that this was what Mommy Muster and Mrs. Edleman were aiming at culturally if not literally, but not achieving. First she took a small Italian earthenware jug out of the refrigerator, and next a frosty stemmed cocktail glass into which she popped an olive. Then she measured gin and vermouth jigger by jigger—"Four to one. I hope you don't mind?" "On the contrary"—swizzled ice, dumped it, put jug and glass on a little silver tray along with a tiny embroidered napkin, carried it back into the living room, bumped into me when she turned around, indicated the wing chair as perhaps more comfortable, which it wasn't, it made me feel as if I had blinders on, ceremoniously poured for both of us, and finally handed me the cocktail glass, tiny napkin, and a little dish of somethings to go with it. Silence settled. I crossed and uncrossed my legs. Gazed at the fire and the picture above it. Nibbled the somethings, which had a cheesy taste to them. Took a sip of my martini. It was still more awkward than those conferences about the humor of Charles Lamb under the absent eye of Dr. Slavitt, and yet like them curiously flattering. Also, though she had told me not to dress and I had more or less taken her word for it, Dr. Lorillard herself was wearing low-cut black taffeta and black peau de soie (?)—right word?—pumps. Even more surprising, in view of the boyish bob and pearls and the gap-toothed ladylike smile, her legs in their sheer black stockings turned out to be sexy and gorgeous.

"You're looking at John's Yale chair," she said, pleased.

I looked where I hadn't been looking. It was only a black wooden spindle-backed armchair with a gold crest on its head slat. I didn't know colleges had chairs —another famous first—did Medaglia have one? Did Medaglia even have a school song? Yes, though no one remembered the words. We had run through it at freshman assembly. If Medaglia did have a chair with a crest would anyone buy it? Maybe that sorority girl to match her blazer. Maybe, the way things were going with her these days, Leonora.

"Whenever John comes home from a trip he goes straight to his Yale chair," Dr. Lorillard said, regarding it affectionately. I took a long sip of my martini—strong, but excellent once you got used to it—and regarded *her* affectionately. Well, at least the reason for the pressing invitation was now apparent. There was no mystery at all. She had asked me to dinner because her husband was away and she was lonesome. A late marriage, she explained, she had been thirty-seven, he almost forty, the first for each and ecstatically happy. "Really?" It was still a bit too intimate, like watching her comb her baby-fine hair, but a lot more fascinating. I was all set to ask her the nature of "John's" trips, but at that point the maid came in bearing my yellow pompons in a vase, like a sudden unwelcome souvenir of my parents, and said sotto voce that dinner was ready. Dr. Lorillard thanked her kindly for the information, thanked me kindly for the flowers, which immediately blended in handsomely with the furniture (dear Dr. Lorillard), and suggested we finish off the "dregs" first. Another lovely idea, though the dregs were so strong that when I rose to "wash up," again at Dr. Lorillard's suggestion, I bumped into a side table and all kinds of little precious objects rattled. Passing through the bedroom to get to the bathroom, I saw a good deal of fresh ironing arranged in neat piles on the bed, and this somehow impressed me most of all. It turned the maid into a kind of female valet.

Much of the conversation at dinner, though not the dinner itself, was lost on me. We had a mixture of tomatoes and onions and chunks of green smooth things in tall parfait glasses. The green things were avocados. I told her I had never tasted an avocado before. Dr. Lorillard cut the steak in strips. I had never seen a steak cut in strips before, but didn't say so. It obviously required a Gentile cut. There were wineglasses and red wine in a decanter. Dr. Lorillard told me more about herself, blurting out the last sentence of unspoken paragraphs, repeating others, and just as in class and in conferences, suddenly blurted out a laugh when nothing funny had been said. Fuzzily, but hanging on to my best manners, I absorbed further details, that she had been born and brought up in Brooklyn Heights, her father a rich and radical trial lawyer, her mother his fourth wife, that on the first day of dancing class Gloria Gould had peed in her pants.

"Peed in her pants!" Dr. Lorillard cried, laughing, as if this were stop-the-presses news. ("Gloria Gould was Jewish," my father said later. "Oh, *Daddy*.") Dr. Lorillard had defied her father and *step*mother (?)—had I heard right?—by refusing to come out at a regular debutante ball and making them settle for a small tea for only thirty instead. "Incredible." "Tea for only thirty!" She had done her graduate work at Oxford in the twenties, which accounted for the velvet beret she wore in academic processions instead of a mortar board, and the ermine lining of her hood. Not real ermine, of course. Mangy spotted rabbit. "Mangy spotted rabbit!" With this we rose and went back to have our coffee and more drinks in the living room.

Somehow, back at the fire, with our demitasses and scotch-and-sodas, the atmosphere became calmer and smoother, more teacher and student. Dr. Lorillard winced at the name of Dr. Slavitt, who came up I'm not sure how, making it permanently clear that it was his manners not his politics that offended her, and quickly went on to the matter of John's cure for his insomnia, "He polishes the brass in the middle of the night," "Oh, charming," and from there proceeded to the best way of cleaning diamonds, "Just dip them in a simple soapy solution," "I'll remember that." She leaned forward.

"Now, tell me about your handsome boyfriend."

I was a bit taken aback. So Gerald and I had been observed? I had assumed that as a couple we were beneath the notice of the faculty.

"Does he drive you back and forth to school?"

"Gerald? No, it's his father's car. He only gets it sometimes, and then he's only allowed to take it as far as Forest Hills."

"Ah. I thought maybe I could get a lift sometimes."

I shook my head. We sipped some more at our scotch-and-sodas.

"And your charming cousin?"

Charming *cousin?* This was really a stopper. I mentally ticked off the slews of them on each side, Morty, Stanley, Irene, Raymond, Mildred, Anna, Izzy, and suddenly realized whom she must mean.

"Is something wrong?"

"I'm suffering from aggravation. . . . No, I mean he doesn't exactly live with us anymore. In fact, he's moved to Brooklyn."

"Brooklyn," Dr. Lorillard said, inclining her head with more than her usual courteous interest. I remembered that her childhood had been spent in Brooklyn Heights. Impossible, even if I were devoted to the truth, to bring up the matter of a furnished room.

"He has these relatives on his mother's side," I said, making a stab at it anyway.

"Mother's side. Of course."

"Also, my brother's coming home soon, and we need his room back."

"Brother coming home soon."

It was time to go, but I wasn't sure how to make my getaway. Whether to offer to help wash up the scotch-and-soda glasses, the tiny demitasse cups and saucers, or what. The maid had left long ago. Dr. Lorillard was smiling, but her eyes were glazed over.

"Somehow I had assumed you were an only child," she said, for some reason achieving one of her few complete sentences of the evening.

"No, I have this brother. He'll have to figure out what to do now. My brother."

"And you? Have you figured out yet what *you* want to do?"

"Pioneer work in Palestine!" I cried out.

I stood up, stumbling into coffee tables, excusing myself to them, thanking her and laughing each time. She helped me on with my coat, explaining that I could either walk the half block to Lexington or ask the doorman to get me a cab.

"Oh, Dr. Lorillard," I said, suddenly turning to her with one arm in my sleeve.

"Elizabeth."

"Elizabeth. You don't know what it is to wake up in this country and not know how you got here."

I had no idea why I had blurted this out. I wasn't sure whether I was sorry or glad. I only knew I didn't want to call her Elizabeth.

Three

1

Josef had turned into a relative, coming for dinner Friday nights, sitting around the house most of Sunday. Gerald had transmogrified into a sort of fiancé, though more in the breach, alas, than in the observance. His mother cordially detested me. His mother's mother, on the other hand, a genteel old thing who wore toques like Queen Mary's, took for granted what nobody else took for granted, and invited me to Schrafft's for tea, where she poured from a leaky pewter pot and passed me tiny little sandwiches with the crusts cut off. She told me about Harlem when she was young. (Brooklyn Heights. Harlem. I was certainly learning the geography of old New York.) Rosalie's boyfriend was on the last lap of his divorce, but still in no position to make a run for it. In other words, a new term, but otherwise a stalemate all around. February, the lowest point of the year, the *"anus anni,"* as Dr. Slavitt put it in his most sardonic, dispirited tone, looking at me with more contempt than ever, as if all I could understand of it was the Latin.

Then Gerald's mother, not feeling too well, went off to the hospital for a few days, during which stay Gerald honored her absence as always with abstinence. "What's the *matter* with her?" I whispered to Gerald during the History of Art course which we were both taking for the two easy credits and sure A. One of the few sure A's in Gerald's life. "Tuma," Gerald wrote in his notebook. "Tumor," I wrote back automatically, before the lights went out and the slides appeared. Gerald and I held hands in the darkness—I had never in my wildest dreams as a straight A student imagined holding hands with a boy while actually in class, so I was thrilled and scared stiff—and then there was a click and a slide of Michelangelo's David. "Oh, my god, that *wrist*," Gerald said, sitting upright. The only time I had seen him so excited before was by Botticelli's St. Sebastian. Maybe St. Theresa in Agony. The lights went on, and he was still practicing that special flex, that arch. Our professor laughed with pleasure to see him. She was a tiny Austrian refugee with a thick accent and a face like a monkey, and an unfortunate habit of wandering into expensive French restaurants with a notebook and trying to settle down to work, assuming them to be cafés. They were near where she lived and called themselves things like Le Bistro, which was what had confused her in the first place. She was always asking us over to her apartment, not like Dr. Lorillard as teacher to student, but because she really thought of us as potential friends, European style. Gerald had gone a few times. I hadn't yet. The thought, though flattering, made me nervous.

The wrist-flexing continued on through Gerald's Greenwich Village production of *The Marriage of Figaro* where he had everybody doing it, Count Almaviva, Figaro, the lackey, Sherwin Schiff prancing around in his tights and red snood, everybody almost except Susannah and the Countess. Cherubino had all she could do just to hang on to her sword and strut. The whole thing was an utter fiasco, redeemed maybe only by the fact that Gerald at least didn't have a *singing* part, and that Milton Schwartz had painted a few marvelous screens as backdrops, pregnant Ruthie assisting. Gerald, of course, thought he had a tremendous success on his hands, and so did his teacher, to judge from the way they bowed repeatedly to our overly enthusiastic applause. Mommy Muster was there too, well out of the hospital, to take pride in her little boy's achievement, and looking none the worse for wear. She had on a silver fox coat, a tiny black hat with a floppy rose perched on her upsweep, and ankle-strapped shoes, and she smiled at me with her mouth closed. I didn't understand why she hated me so. Luke Lazar's mother liked me. Rosalie's mother liked me. Her own mother liked me. And I was always on the lookout for a mother, so to speak. But there it was, or rather there *she* was, casting a pall over the proceedings. She insisted on going home alone, leaving "you children to enjoy yourselves." We made a tired stab at a cast party in the Jumble Shop and then all went home too, I ironically to an empty house. It was Washington's Birthday and my parents had gone to Lakewood for the weekend with Josef.

2

The next afternoon, a dark and snowy Saturday, Gerald came over as planned. I immediately and urgently started to pull out my sofa bed. He watched me, still keeping his coat on.

"Listen," Gerald said, "how about a hot chocolate at Rumpelmayer's first?"

Hot chocolate at Rumpelmayer's? It was a lovely idea. Gerald did have lovely ideas, though at the moment he was frowning for some reason. Romantic but chancy. My parents weren't due back until tomorrow, but they could still surprise us by coming home unexpectedly tonight. They had done it before when they were worried about my being alone, and this time of year sundown came perilously early. Nevertheless I decided it was worth the risk. I pushed back my sofa bed. A walk along Central Park South, holding gloved hands with Gerald under a leaden winter sky, madly, passionately in love, aching with desire, loving the ache, loving the suspense of it, knowing that *soon* . . . Oh, yes, I would always remember right now, like those first days in the Village. The Plaza fountain hove into view, and we turned in at Rumpelmayer's elegant display window with its creased red velvet and empty bonbon boxes tied with gold ribbon. The waitress brought us two cups of purply chocolate, delicately frothing at the top.

"Mommy asked me if you always dressed like that," Gerald remarked quite casually, spooning away at his froth.

"Dressed like what?"

"You know, the way you did last night."

I looked down at myself, astonished. Dressed like *what?* True, it was almost always wholesale, either from Lowyse Frocks or a friend of my father's partner. But always the plainest numbers, no matter how much urging otherwise. That is, Rosalie I could understand, god forgive me, not that Mommy Muster with her silver fox and ankle-straps was in a position to criticize. But *me?*

"I asked Leonora and she said yes you did."

Leonora? Leonora the cow? That super-bovine intellectual? When had she ever deigned to talk to the likes of Gerald? When had he ever thought of addressing a word to her? But now it seemed they were not only in cahoots but passing judgment on me. Where? In the Medaglia cafeteria?

I put down my cup and stared at him, but Gerald, quite unmoved, certainly by the possibility of having hurt my feelings, went on to a subject that evidently meant much more to him: should we buy a pair of subscriptions to the New Friends of Music next season? It was like his idea of having hot chocolate at Rumpelmayer's. Distracting, soothing, unutterably romantic, and with a sense of continuity to it. Town Hall on Sunday evenings, listening to string quartets at dusk, holding hands with Gerald on a regular subscription basis. We walked over to the bus by way of Fifty-seventh

Street, and as the snow suddenly fell fast, I held his hand tightly, practically pulling off his glove when he stopped to look at the posters outside of Carnegie Hall. Leopold Stokowski conducting Bach's Toccata and Fugue in D Minor. Next door, at the recital hall, the usual debuts, a girl soprano, a boy pianist. There were throwaways for them in the music room at Medaglia. Back home, I tossed aside cushions and pulled at bedsprings as fast as I could, merely glancing over my shoulder, as Gerald started to unbutton me, at a Victorian picture book which lay face up on my night table. A present from Gerald, who found it in a second-hand bookstore. *Children of Yesteryear*, it was called, and they all had rosy cheeks and wore things like ermine muffs and violets. Outside it was still snowing heavily and almost unbearably romantic, but though it was my room and not his, and no Mommy involved, and Gerald had got down to his socks, he still seemed reluctant. In fact, I glanced at the picture book again, to tell the truth he always seemed reluctant, and had ever since those first two times in the little room on Eighth Street. I didn't understand it, having been brought up so thoroughly to believe that a man only wanted one thing of you and that once he had it he abandoned you forever. Viz., Betty Rubin's story of having gone off to a hotel in Philadelphia with her latest fiancé and climbed into bed with him naked. But then, as Betty proudly put it, she changed her mind and for the rest of the night he "respected" her. Yet here was Gerald, so devoted, so dependable in his fashion, more so than Robert who wouldn't have walked in the snow to save his life, so full of presents, mostly bits of Victoriana but also flowers. And here was I, grappling, pleading, cajoling this big beautiful hulk of a boy, who was there but not there. I forgot the rest. As always it was wonderful, as always he gave me a thrilling little kiss at the end. As always I adored him.

"Your eyes are beautiful," he said, looking down at me from above. "Coming does something to the eyes." He climbed off and lay beside me. I leaned on one elbow the better to admire him. But Gerald turned the other way.

"Look, I have something to tell you," he said.

"What, darling? What's the matter?"

"I'm gay."

"You certainly don't look it. You look depressed, in fact."

"Queer," Gerald said. "Homosexual."

I laughed with relief. I had been worried about another girl, the one tall enough to dance cheek to cheek with him, in fact.

"Oh, darling," I said. "That's such a common adolescent guilt feeling. It doesn't mean anything. You won't believe this, but I've had the same worries about myself." It was better not to say concerning whom. "What happened? Did you have a crush on a teacher? Play doctor with another little boy?"

"I'm a homosexual," Gerald said.

"Darling, darling," I said. "You're imagining things."

He wasn't imagining anything. The boy, as Gerald himself would have put it, was as queer as a nine-dollar bill. Still, I refused to believe it. I told him it was a passing fancy, a phase that would go away as he got older. In retaliation, and when I didn't have too much homework, he began to take me all over, to haunts on Lexington and Third. Bars teeming with handsome young men and boys, older men who looked like aging movie stars, all ogling each other. I still couldn't believe it, it was such a waste. Gerald made me go in and I sat there in semi-darkness with my rye and ginger ale being the only girl in a situation that ought to have been thrilling but wasn't because they were all glaring at Gerald for having brought me. He told me, laughing, what went on in the bathrooms, and this I categorically refused to believe. Then we cruised up and down the avenue some more. Cruise. It was part of a whole new vocabulary that Gerald was teaching me. Cruise. Trade, that was Gerald, not yet confirmed but up for grabs. The older, tired men, poor things, were queens. He told me how many musicians, movie stars, stage actors, sailors, truck drivers, sports heroes, ballet dancers were queer. Definitely musicians. You definitely had to whore around to get anywhere in the music world. "Oh, Gerald," I said. But he had already gone on to the subject of bare-ass beach on Fire Island and the fact that you could be picked up by somebody any place, any time, sleep with him the whole night, and not even know his name when you left in the morning. "Sex is no introduction," Gerald said, tee-heeing. He also told me that in the Navy, where he had first been seduced ("So that's how it happened, poor darling"), the acknowledged offenders were slapped in the brig, and the loudspeaker would blare at mealtimes, *"Homos, muster for chow!"* But somehow his obsessive delight in telling me all these things backfired. Queer, queer, queer. The whole world was queer. He began to sound like my mother when she looked up from the *Forward* to tell me who was Jewish. But who could I tell about Gerald? Rosalie? No. Milton Schwartz? Definitely not. It would ruin their friendship. Besides, it was just a question of trying to cure him. We went on sleeping with each other as much, or rather as little as before, in his father's car, pulled off on a side road in Westchester, on my sofa bed when my parents were away, and to tell the truth there was a very attractive quality to Gerald's reluctance. It was so much more exciting than being pawed by some boy like Robert, who was always trying to make you.

4

Obviously, the last person I would think of telling *anything* was Leonora, so when she suddenly invited me to her house to meet her fiancé, it was even more of a shock than seeing that engagement ring in the first place. I was still sore about the clothes business, but out of curiosity I went anyhow. From the moment I got there, it was clear that both Herman and Mr. Edleman were odd men out. Herman was very nice and very cordial. He didn't even look like a Herman, except that he wore glasses and his hair was parted maybe a little bit more toward the middle than the side. Mr. Edleman was very nice too, though I don't know how many times Leonora and Martin called him "Izzy" just to put him in his place. Yes, Martin was actually there from the beginning, on the spot, in person. A further shock, partly on account of that uncanny, astounding resemblance to Leonora, and partly because though I always thought of Martin as terribly snotty, he wasn't even really rude. It was just that aura that Leonora and Mrs. Edleman created around him. Martin was brilliant, Martin was handsome. Martin could do no wrong. And, of course, anything Leonora could do Martin could do better. Which was the rub, the terrible rub. He even, as if to prove the point, had a pair of married friends with him, married not like Milton and Ruthie, or like the future Leonora and Herman, but exemplars, as it were, of what marriage with Martin Edleman would be when the time came. The young man, Dick, a former fellow Air Force officer now in tweeds with a pipe, the girl Susan in a beautiful pale plaid skirt and a blue English cashmere sweater. (Was this how Gerald wanted me to dress? But Leonora didn't dress this way, nor Mommy Muster, either; you had to be born to it, also be tall with a flat stomach.) Dick and Susan had a red convertible waiting for them downstairs, top up on account of the cold March weather, and they were even at that moment on their way back to it, underscoring the point that happy as they were to see Martin's family, they had far better things to do than just hang around. Martin had greeted me cordially, as usual as if we had just met, and as usual before leaving remarked, "She looks just like Phoebe White, doesn't she?" As usual Leonora agreed, and so did Dick and Susan, except that this time, for some reason, I noticed that Martin had hair growing out of his ears.

When the three of them were gone, Leonora got very dim. She had a bad cold, and now retreated to a corner armchair near where the Christmas tree had been, muffling her face with a handkerchief. The little diamond on her finger sparkled every time she sneezed. But poor Herman, its author, sparkled not at all. Everybody had smiled at him a great deal, Martin, the smart-set young marrieds, "Izzy," who paternally and awkwardly put his hand on Herman's shoulder from time to time. But only Mrs. Edleman spoke to him directly, and then of matters she must have already mentioned a thousand times, like the pastel portraits "of the children when they were small." I was very tempted to mention Dr. Lorillard's genuine Mary Cassatt, but that would have been playing Leonora's game, and I felt too sorry for Herman to do that. Like Gerald's St. Sebastian, he must already have been repeatedly pierced by a thousand slings and arrows, in this case tiny twitting references to matters "Jamesian," Mozart's Köchel listings, asked in astonishment that, what, he had never heard of the *Dichte Liebe?* Leonora kept on sneezing, and somehow the more she sneezed the more I saw poor Herman as a prisoner there, deluded and bound in some way before he could understand what had happened. I felt that it was up to me to save him, except that I felt like a prisoner too. And why had they asked *me* to see their captured specimen? Why not Maria? Why not Betty Rubin? In fact, why show him off at all? We talked a little of this and that, and of course technically Leonora *had* caught herself an Ivy League graduate, that is Herman *had* gone to the University of Pennsylvania, if only to the Wharton School of Business. Ah, yes, the best school of business in the country, I understood. More smiles. More silence. Leonora sneezed.

"I hear Lorillard gave you an A-plus on that paper," Leonora said nasally, eyes tearing.

Trust Leonora to bring *that* up. How had she heard? I had kept it a dark secret.

"But of course there are more important things, aren't there?" Mrs. Edleman said smiling, quickly intercepting.

Was that it then? Were they trying to tell me that marriage was more important than grades? No, that might have been Mrs. Edleman but it wasn't Leonora. Grades were beneath Leonora. Besides, the whole joy, the whole beauty of Gerald, in every sense of the word, was that I had absolutely no desire to marry him. Marriage was out of the question. For the first time in my life, I didn't wake up with the nightmare of the catered affair.

More awkward silence. Mr. Edleman picked up a

copy of *The Saturday Evening Post* from the coffee table, glanced at the Norman Rockwell cover of a little boy in a barbershop, leafed through it, put it down again. A copy of the *Gorham Review* lay next to it. There was a poem featured on the cover by a famous poet named George Auerbach, whom I had never heard of.

"Oh, yes, Leonora liked it there very much," Mrs. Edleman said, nodding and smiling in answer to an unasked question. "But then she became ill, and we wanted her close to us."

Christ, it suddenly seemed to me, what a sad girl was Leonora.

5

Still, it was incredible when Maria called with the news, though of course such news was her specialty. Leonora had gone mad. Literally. They had found her sitting on one of the lions in front of the New York Public Library. Oh, god. It was only a joke I had made to cheer myself up. I didn't mean it. Though trust Leonora to be so intellectual to the end. They had carted her off to Payne Whitney singing, "Give a cheer for the Jones Junior High." This I absolutely couldn't understand. Obviously it was rooted in her psyche. Nevertheless, the news obsessed me. I was terrified. I could hardly focus on anything else. I sat through the whole Easter show at Radio City with Gerald and Rosalie and Sherwin Schiff, watching *The Late George Apley*, then a chorus line of nuns waving their calla lilies to *Kamenoi Ostrow*, and thinking no, no, no, it's simply not possible. I mean, she was my friend even if I hated her, I had talked to her by the hour, I had slept over, she had shaken my hand bed-to-bed, brought me a little souvenir bottle of violet perfume from Canada, insulted me, scorned me, switched records on me so that I had emoted through the exact same movement of the Rachmaninoff Piano Concerto twice without knowing it. We had understood each other, or at least understood the terms of the conflict. And now, if she was crazy—schizophrenic, in fact—what did that make *me?* Oh, no, Leonora the Weird, not *that* weird. As the days and weeks went on, Maria supplied more and more details, savoring each one, her face growing more and more heart-shaped. Leonora had handed in a midterm paper in Philosophy that spoke in two voices, each line alternating with the other. Martin had been thrown out of graduate school for plagiarism and there was now talk of his going into business with their father. The shame of Martin's disgrace plus being engaged to Herman, not to mention maybe being pregnant, had told on her and she had finally cracked. They were giving her insulin shock treatments that turned her hair dark and erased her memory. We were to show no surprise when we saw her. We didn't. There she sat on her bed in Payne Whitney seemingly very pleased to see Maria and me when we came in. True, her hair was not only darker, almost rust-colored, but cut short. She was much fatter. But the conversation went pleasantly enough. There was nothing crazy about her. This was worse than anything. To be crazy and not be crazy. Maria came home to dinner with me, and my brother Walter, who was now at a separation center, asked her for a date. To my surprise she accepted. They went out several times, in fact. Walter also took out Betty Rubin, who didn't speak to me again for about a week.

On account of Leonora, many of us started to go to psychiatrists on the sly, paying for them out of our allowances. I went to one recommended by Leonora's own analyst—Mrs. Edleman was only too gracious about giving me the name and address—who sent me to a bushy-browed Viennese, who in turn sent me off to take a battery of Rorschach tests in which I saw only black bats and creatures balancing on precipices. He clearly had trouble with the language, he was never going to understand my English, particularly colloquialisms and idiomatic expressions, not to mention hypercorrectness, as I explained to him repeatedly. Nevertheless, at the end of each session, handing him ten dollars in cash—irony, it was the same amount as a week's rent for the little room in the Village—I would turn back and ask, "Aren't you going to say, 'God bless you, my child'?" Rosalie had the same trouble with hers. Her mother was picking up the tab. They were always either listening in silence, or answering questions with a question.

Leonora was now allowed out on weekends. One Sunday evening Gerald and I saw her during an intermission of a New Friends of Music concert at Town

Hall. In the hospital, she had looked normal. Now in the crowded lobby she looked like a visitor from another planet. In the jostling, and cries of greeting and general smoky confusion, it was hard to say more than a few words to her. "The last Rasoumovsky was especially good, wasn't it?" I said, trying to keep things on a normal keel. "Rasoumovsky?" "Quartet." "What quartet?" Leonora asked pleasantly. Back in our seats, I started to say something to Gerald, but he shushed me with his finger. I kept looking around for Leonora, and couldn't find her. Milton was there with poor Myrna and a very pregnant Ruthie, Sherwin Schiff was at the side of an aging composer who was wearing pancake makeup, Maria Dolorosa sat next to a handsome date, smiling at the stage mournfully, like a misplaced Mona Lisa. But where was Leonora? Had she come alone? With her brother? With Herman? I could barely listen to the Debussy, let alone swoon to it as I usually did, especially when sitting next to Gerald.

"Darling—?" I started to say, as the final applause broke out, but he, who usually rushed to his feet, clapping wildly, crying bravo, uncharacteristically began to push me ahead of him through the crowded aisle, ignoring the crush in the lobby, the excited greetings, the exclamations, the cries about *"Axel! . . . Sasha! . . . Lenny!"* Gerald was excited too, but curiously determined to get out of there. He kept his hand firmly under my elbow until we were safe at Schrafft's. Gerald loved that particular Schrafft's. It was the same one his grandmother had taken me to. They seemed to regard it as another piece of old New York.

"God, it was really creepy to see Leonora," I said, watching Gerald dig into his ice-cream soda. "I mean what are they doing for her? Those shocks to the brain. They can't be good. They must be destroying her intelligence, which, when you think about it, is really all she's got. She's certainly not gifted, she's certainly not beautiful—even though she does imagine she has this terrific taste in clothes—" It was a stupid dig and I hurried over it, particularly since Gerald seemed not to have heard. He was still busy with his soda. All black, unusual for him. I was going to ask him if he had ever heard of Phoebe White and changed my mind.

"I don't know," I said finally. "I'm really losing my faith in psychiatry. Dr. Hamburger doesn't even say anything back and that's at ten dollars an hour. And look at what they've done to Leonora. You talk to her about a concert and she doesn't even know she's heard a concert. It's incredible. Frankly, Gerald, I used to think you should go to one too, but now—"

"I am going," Gerald said, asking me if I were going to finish the rest of my apple pie.

"Going where?"

"To a psychiatrist," Gerald said, swapping plates. It was a peculiar point of honor with him, not stacking up empties so that the waitress would know how much he had eaten. He also apologized whenever he buttered his bread whole, even for a sandwich, since his mother had taught him to break it up first into little pieces.

"A psychiatrist? Really? But since when? Who is he?"

"She," Gerald said.

A woman. Yes, that made sense. You were supposed to transfer to the opposite sex, though Leonora's own psychiatrist was a woman too. On the other hand, Leonora was certifiably mad. Still, why hadn't he told me? What was she like?

"About thirty-five. A Negro," Gerald said.

A *Negro?* Woman I had just understood. Made myself understand. But a Negro? Wouldn't that complicate matters? Make them, God forgive me, terribly murky? Also, I had heard lately that far from turning people away from being queer, psychiatrists were now trying to have them adjust to it. What good would that do me? Having Gerald adjusted to being queer when my whole aim in life was to convert him?

"Listen," I said, "I'm almost positive my parents are going back to Lakewood this weekend with my cousin —if not, they're almost sure to go to Miami at the end of the month."

Gerald laughed and shook his head. A real laugh, with pride in it. "Not a chance. I've got the clap."

Gonorrhea? But that was a wartime disease. I thought unwillingly of my brother Walter.

"Are you *sure?*" I said. "Who did you get it from?"

"An opera singer," Gerald said, swapping plates again and sipping from an empty straw.

I looked around Schrafft's, with its anti-Semitic Irish waitresses and lace paper doilies. Some old New York.

"An opera singer," I said bitterly. "Lovely. Tenor or baritone?"

"Soprano."

"A *soprano?* Who the hell *is* she?"

"Oh, I'm not telling you," Gerald said, tittering.

"Now listen here, Gerald," I said. "I'm sorry. The other is one thing. But if you're going to have an affair with a woman, I want to know who it is. I have a right to know."

"Glenda Green," Gerald said.

"But she was Queen of the Night at the City Center. She was in the lobby before. She's hideous."

Gerald agreed.

"She looks like a pig. She has a nose like a snout. She's obese."

"With tits down to her belly button," Gerald said, laughing some more. "And you know how I love tits. I have to close my eyes before I dive in."

My head was whirling. *Why? Why?*

"But I told you in the beginning," Gerald said, now sober with surprise. "You have to whore if you want to get somewhere in the music world."

"I don't believe you," I said. "She's disgusting. You have to give her up. I won't stand for this."

Gerald's handsome black eyebrows drew together in confusion and then in anger. I suddenly realized why he had shoved me out of Town Hall by the elbow. It wasn't that he hadn't wanted me to see Glenda Green. He hadn't wanted her to see *me.*

6

I gave him until the first seder to give her up. The Negro psychiatrist told him she understood my feelings, but he was not to answer to ultimatums. Gerald duly reported this, as well as other bulletins. How repulsive Glenda was in bed, those big tits, that sex smell as of rotten fish. I don't think he understood why this bothered me any more than he understood why women minded rape. On the night of the first seder he called to say that his psychiatrist, Nelda, had *definitely* said that he was not to respond to ultimatums. Therefore . . . I looked around the table, at my brother Walter on leave from the separation center, at my cousin Josef, at an impecunious aunt, a few of her paltry children, my bustling mother seated for a moment, my father reclining against pillows, wondering if this was all life had in store for me, and in the light of the holiday candles scooped up matzo crumbs with a broken heart.

7

It was amazing, however, that life not only resumed, it actually picked up. There was, of course, the usual spring-break descent from Cornell by Robert, and the visit to his sister and her boyfriend and the necking to the slide and thump of the concealed Capehart. I wondered, as we grappled in the self-service elevator, if he knew I was no longer a virgin. Maybe he did, maybe he didn't. In any case, it was clear that he didn't want our habits disturbed. He invited me, however, to his Senior Prom in June. I accepted, though it was a peculiar departure from principle for a boy who refused to live in a dorm like other boys or join a fraternity. Where would I stay? In his room at his boardinghouse. He would sleep on the sofa. Come to think of it, maybe Robert didn't think I was a virgin after all.

More interestingly, Luke Lazar, though he adored his family, not only his mother and the silly ladies with whom she played canasta—"Adorable!"—but also his father, a man-about-town who once took us for a drink to the Café de la Paix where a heavily made-up woman in spike heels and a silver fox jacket greeted him all too familiarly—"Marry him," Mr. Lazar said hurriedly to change the subject, as Luke laughed, "I'll pay for the maid"—this same Luke was the first one of us who actually left home. He took an apartment with a friend, another boy in the chorus of *Annie Get Your Gun*. It was a walk-up in the Eighties on Park Avenue, and since his friend had been stationed in France, the night I came we ate pears and cheese and wine. I had never eaten fruit and cheese before, but it turned out to be an interesting and delicious combination. There was also a young psychiatrist there that night, whom I liked at once. In a funny way he reminded me of Gerald. Not that there was any real resemblance, physical or otherwise, but he *talked* to me. There was no hint of any future grappling in the self-service elevator. Even when he showed me his new office a few blocks away, with the brand-new couch only too evident and awaiting use of some kind or other, he spoke mainly of his own analysis, which he was still in—this surprised me, I thought you had to be all finished before they let you work on patients. How did this apply to the horrible Hamburger?—his hopes for building up a practice, his interest in the theater. Would I care to see *Annie Get Your Gun* with him? Certainly. It had evidently escaped him that being a friend of Luke's I might have seen it already, that I might want to see something serious, like *All My Sons*, or *Another Part of the Forest*. What? Dinner beforehand? At the Harvard Club? Absolutely. ("You see?" I said triumphantly to Dr. Hamburger. "No transference. Not to you, anyway. He's a *date*.") When my parents asked who was picking me up and I said a psychiatrist I had met at Luke's I was greeted with only mild approval. They liked the idea of dates, all right, but not the idea of anybody, boys included, which meant Luke, who went to live on their own. Also, I could see that the word "psychiatrist" didn't sit too well with my father. "He's a doctor," I explained to my mother, bypassing him. "An M.D. A specialist." "Specialist?" my mother said, tilting her head and pursing her lips with interest. My father remained stony. "A Harvard graduate," I told him. He relented a little, especially after an exchange of gentlemanly handshakes when Bart rang the doorbell. Something told me not to mention that Dr. Slavitt was also a Harvard graduate, though I doubted that either of my parents would have known who he was to begin with. They weren't ever interested in the process, only the result.

Bart did indeed take me to dinner at the Harvard Club, seeing me in through the Ladies' Entrance. We sat under the picture of Henry Hoare, and he told me the joke about Hoare House. It was all very Lorillard, a place of waiters and white linen and good drinks and somber portraits, very much the real thing. So much for Mommy Muster and her Schrafft's and tearooms. I was getting tired of *Annie Get Your Gun*, and still wishing we had seen *Another Part of the Forest* instead, but didn't say so, and tried not to remember standing in this same lobby during intermission with Gerald, not to mention what happened afterward. At least we didn't go backstage or anything to wait for Luke and watch him pathetically pretend to be an important member of the cast. At the end of the evening Bart escorted me to my door, rang for the elevator, shook my hand, thanked me for a pleasant evening and said he would call again soon. Which he did.

So that yes, actually, in spite of the misery and the loneliness, and almost against my will, it was a very busy time for me socially. I even double-dated with Maria and a *young* garment manufacturer she had dug up for me named Harold. Maria's date, Julius, who worked at the YMHA in some sort of publicity capacity, at present touting a left-handed violinist, was clearly wild about her. Harold fell for me immediately. He said that as soon as the weather got warmer, he would take me out to a driving range and teach me golf. I don't know why this depressed me almost as much as the fact that he was lighting a cigar when he made the invitation, turning it wetly in his mouth to catch the flame, but it did. Maybe it reminded me of last summer when I was visiting Maria and her parents at their cottage on Long Island and her stepfather offered to teach me golf too. I was very good at it, a natural. Maria was furious. The weekend wasn't supposed to have anything to do with her vulgar family or their vulgar cottage or their country club. It was so ironic that the smitten Julius never dreamed that Maria actually detested him, and certainly would never have believed what Maria had in mind the night she led me into the black dunes behind the house to show me "the ocean."

I decided to go see Leonora, who was now living in a hotel for women, on the advice of the doctors at Payne Whitney. She was fatter and less Alice in Wonderland than ever, but seemingly content. "You really like it here?" I asked. "Oh, yes," Leonora said, with that new smile which was both unbecoming and uncharacteristic. She had been one of the bitches of the century, after all, illness notwithstanding. The walls were curiously bare. She was not allowed to deface them, either with thumbtacks or Scotch tape—ergo no pictures. This didn't bother her either, nor did the fact that she wasn't supposed to see her parents, though they footed the bill, all the bills. I didn't understand the reasoning. If the Edlemans supported her, how was she independent of them? Weren't they in effect subsidizing her to spit in their eye? I asked my psychiatrist about this and he asked why I was asking. So yes, indeed, it was wonderful in terms of transference alone that instead of that brick wall who didn't even understand English, I had Bart, whom I still saw and with whom I went to the Met, sitting down (*Manon,* all five acts), *Swan Lake* by the Ballet Theater, *real* ballet, though it was given at the City Center, dined in fine restaurants, and who in return never laid a glove on me. "A regular gentleman," my mother said, having it now firmly fixed in her head that she was dealing with not only a doctor but a specialist.

In gratitude, or maybe general retaliation, or maybe sheer loneliness, half looking for Gerald though I saw him at school from a distance, I took her to *the* Schrafft's, ready to pounce if she said so much as one word about tea in a glass, and why were the sandwiches so small with practically nothing in them? After all, this was a woman who didn't even know her own birthday. But in fact she behaved like a perfect lady, very neat and curious in her printed blue silk dress and cameo brooch, and even with her broken English a thousand times more ladylike than Mrs. Muster, only picking up little lids of bread so as to peer at the fillings and avoid the meat—I didn't tell her one of them was spiced ham, and out of deference didn't eat it myself—smiling at the nasty Irish waitress who gave us our check. She was so terribly pleased I had brought her there, I felt awful, and though I automatically started to go Dutch as I did with Gerald, she of course wouldn't hear of it and paid for us both out of a little change purse. Why did I keep forgetting that she was my mother? That she thought of herself as my mother?

The next day, still on the lookout for Gerald—why not admit it?—I went to our monkey-faced art teacher's house. There was more cheese and fruit and wine. I had begun to associate this with brownstones, though Dr. Geoffrey's brownstone was not at all like Luke Lazar's but a place that had been longer lived in, furnished to suit. Two enormous high-ceilinged rooms with a little kitchen passageway in between, one room looking out on the street, the other on a tree-filled courtyard. Both were furnished identically with prints and etchings and two huge double daybeds, on which one lolled back against a plethora of pillows, feet out, or tucked underneath, but never quite sitting up straight or lying down. There was a very handsome young man named Quentin who was also visiting, and Dr. Geoffrey's husband, also young, if not quite handsome, maybe ten years younger than his wife, but of the same neurasthenic type, and also of the arts, in a manner of speaking. What he did was decorate windows for Bonwit Teller, which was high-toned enough for me, though of course on another level. (Lowyse Frocks could never sell its line to them.) Mr. Geoffrey—Allan—Allan was very courteous and nice, acting like a visitor in his wife's room. I gathered it was *her* room, the one on the courtyard, that we were sprawled in. Allan left, and then after a while, the young man Quentin. "He likes you," Dr. Geoffrey said, meaning Quentin, and I said thank you, though I hadn't liked *him* at all, finding him opaque, and never figuring out whose friend he was or what he did, if anything. She was drinking only white wine, yet her eyes were as glazed over as if it were martinis. Again I heard the story of one of my teacher's lives, this time about a girlhood in Austria—somehow Austria sounded better than Germany, less full of Nazis. In any case Dr. Geoffrey had known nothing about them and still took no interest in politics. She came from a tiny town in the mountains, dotted with beautiful churches, which was what had introduced her to beauty and art—and when not looking at baroque paintings and statuary, was shushing and slaloming amid beautiful snowcapped peaks. So, of course, what was she to make of this strange new country, snowless except for gray slush, uncultivated, and without even a decent café? Since I had never been to Europe I could only guess what she was talking about. Also, I was desperately trying to get off that enormous daybed, inching my way forward and more or less flailing like a turtle, at the same time trying to keep my skirt down. There was something very depressing about her, which I couldn't account for since the whole time she was laughing gaily. "He likes you," she repeated of Quentin, and again I said thank you though I still didn't know what he was about.

Like a lemming, I wended my way back to Schrafft's for tea, now openly looking for Gerald or anything pertaining to him, even his grandmother, though I had forsworn him forever. As I ate my way through the four tiny little tea sandwiches, including, with a certain guilty defiance, the one with the spiced ham, a young man at the next table smiled and struck up a conversation. It was entirely safe, not a pickup. He was married, wearing a wedding ring, and utterly conventional, with blond hair, rimless eyeglasses, and a gray pin-striped business suit. We talked about the weather, the lateness of spring, the fact that there didn't seem to be much spring anymore. He saw me looking at his wedding ring. "Would you like to see a picture of my wife?" he suddenly asked. Indeed I would. He withdrew from his wallet a photograph of a *dark*-haired young man with rimless eyeglasses and a pin-striped business suit. "He's lovely," I said.

8

Luckily, Rosalie called that night with some very exciting news. She was actually going to make her debut at a nightclub in the Village. It had come through very rapidly and unexpectedly via a connection of Luke Lazar's, some agent interested in fostering young talent. It was her big chance, *our* big chance, I thought, though I didn't say so. It was her show after all. "I'm going to puke," Rosalie said, and I told her she wasn't, feeling pretty sick myself with the excitement of it all. But it was a dream come true, the justification of all our wildest hopes and yearnings. "This Saturday? I mean, Rosie, it's practically straight out of a Deanna Durbin movie." "Life imitates art," Rosalie said, which made her more nauseous. She hung up soon after.

I went by myself, wanting to be alone, wanting to experience the full beauty of it without worrying about a date. It was a much bigger place than I had expected, practically barnlike, bigger than Café Society Downtown or the Village Vanguard. They seated me on a kind of balcony in the rear, at a table full of grown-up strangers, flashy Broadway types, also invited, as was clear from their conversation, by the agent. I ordered a rye and ginger ale, and though they just looked me over and went on talking to each other, I wasn't lonely at all. There was going to be a party at Luke Lazar's later in case I needed company, and meanwhile all my energy and attention were focused on Rosalie. The stage was distant and everyone was talking. The talking got louder and more diffuse. It was difficult to concentrate. I suffered through a lousy comedian whom I couldn't hear. "Oh, my *god*," said one of the hennaed ladies at my table, rubbing her forehead with a hand on which red nail polish and a diamond and ruby pinky ring figured prominently. Another round of drinks. A roll of drums. The MC stepped proudly forward. An incoherent, practically inaudible introduction. Then, *"Miss Greer Garson!"* he announced. Gasps, a burst of applause. I was laughing in advance. Of course it was Rosalie, in the hilarious outfit we had all dreamed up together in case she ever got a chance to do Luke's material, little imagining the chance would come so soon. Black turban with droopy iridescent cock feathers, black slinky gown with lots of fake multicolored jewelry covering her poitrine, an outfit that didn't look all that different, come to think of it, from what she wore to class. She placed her hand grandly on the piano, letting loose the long red chiffon handkerchief attached to her high school ring, and took a step forward. Usually it was Luke who accompanied her, but he was over at the Imperial working, and this was some tired sallow guy from the nightclub. I waited for the familiar lines—the lament of a French duchess whose "château" has seen better days —and looked around the table, soon to say that she was my friend, that we went to school together. "Oh, Jesus," said the lady with the flashy pinky ring, covering her face again. I didn't blame her. Not only could we not exactly hear Rosalie, what we did hear made no sense. Waiters circulated with drinks. People began chattering again. It had been wrong and stupid to introduce her as Greer Garson. It aroused expectations, and there was only Rosalie. I didn't say she was my friend. I didn't say a word. I just sat there dismally for a while and then went out and found a cab going uptown. But how could what had looked so great at Medaglia be so amateurish here? She wasn't even a flop, she wasn't anything.

The party at Luke's was already loud and in full swing when I got there, and since it wasn't especially in honor of Rosalie, there were no hard feelings on her account. In fact, when Luke finally did show up, he was even more ebullient than usual. A performance did that to him. "Dearest heart!" he cried when he saw me. Aside from Luke, I didn't really know anyone, except Bart, whom I had met there in the first place. They were all drinking gin, which I disliked, having been trained by my father to stick to scotch or rye as safer, smoking a lot, sometimes mysteriously ducking outside to do so. There was chatter about the Yale Drama School, and the dance, and lots of "darlings" from both sexes. A bunch of them had made a circle around a wild-eyed man with bushy hair and huge spectacles and a beard. A crazy poet, who had been let out of the insane asylum for the weekend. "What's so hot about *that?*" I asked Bart, who had appeared at my side. But he only smiled and disappeared again. For lack of anything better to do, I wandered out into the hallway where a group of people were leaning over the stairwell and puffing out terribly acrid smoke. "Tea," Rosalie's boyfriend said, standing there in his suede jacket—"What?" "Marijuana"—and laughingly asked if I had the nerve to try it. I said I never took a dare and went back inside. Rosalie had also materialized in the interim, and was sitting in the middle of a crowded sofa. I sat down beside her as soon as there was an opening. She had changed into one of her party getups, a fuchsia number with sequins and spangles, that looked more like a costume than her costume, and more out of place, oddly, than if she were wearing it in the cafeteria. Her mascara was very smudged.

"You were great, Rosie," I said, not surprised when she didn't even bother to reply. She took a puff from her long cigarette holder, and then we looked forlornly out into the room, smiling from time to time at no one in particular. Her boyfriend, Sam, was part of a group near the mantelpiece. I didn't like him. He was too sophisticated, too smooth, too old for Rosalie. And then there was the matter of the legal separation. None of us, except for Milton, was even married much less on the verge of divorce. Ironically, Rosalie's mother adored him. She considered him a man of the world, and was extremely gracious and in her element the time he took her and Rosalie to the Russian Tearoom for dinner, then pressed money on the taxi driver for their long haul back to the Bronx. But of course she didn't know his actual circumstances, and Rosalie still hadn't mentioned her ultimate plans. By now, several of what I assumed to be male dancers were holding hands. A few even began to neck openly. One of them leaned over a chair where a man sat whose back was to me. They kissed long and passionately. Then they came up for air and sauntered off together toward the bedroom. A normal couple, except that they were both men, and the one in the chair turned out to be my psychiatrist boyfriend, Bart.

"How dare you people presume to treat innocent *people!*" I cried.

"I'm wondering," Dr. Hamburger said, "why you feel you have to attack *me?*"

Four

1

I wished that *somebody* in my house would try to act surprised that Gerald had popped up again. But everybody, even my mother, took him in their stride, though she kept repeating the word "specialist" over and over again, and shaking her head. "Leave her alone," my father said, sensing I don't know what. In fact, after shouting a few more times at my bushy-browed Viennese, I did go out with Bart again. We went to the Harvard Club for dinner as if nothing had happened, and sat in the old world dining room under the picture of Henry Hoare. Bart made the joke about Hoare House and asked me what I wanted to drink. "An old-fashioned," I said, drawing on what Gerald had taught me, "and leave out the fruit." "Ouch, okay," Bart said. For the sake of a kind of transferred transference—I was still not going to fall in love with the horrible Hamburger—and also spite, I went out with a few more psychiatrists, friends of Bart and Luke Lazar. Straight: I could tell the difference by now. But I was still always uneasy, worried about their suddenly leaning over to kiss sailors, make love to truck drivers in their cabs. Because was it true what the look on Maria's face hinted these days—and how her face hinted these days —that for smart sensitive girls, the only available boys were fags?

With Gerald it was back to Schrafft's and Greenwich Village. Also, his mother was in the hospital for good now. The tumor was malignant and she was dying. "Oh, Gerald!" It was horrible. Obsessively horrible, because as in the case of Leonora, I hated her. A lot of the fathers had died so far—in high school one friend after another would call with the news. In Medaglia there were Milton, Maria, Rosalie, all fatherless too, though Maria had that much despised stepfather, innocent except for his love of gin rummy and golf. I could hardly look at my own father without a pang sometimes, kissing him again on the back of his seamed neck for no reason, and causing him to look around with surprise. (Though once I dreamed he had put me in an arena to be shot with slings and arrows for the benefit of the B'Nai B'rith.) But this was the first mother, and it was so inexorable. The awfulness after Gerald told me kept dawning and dawning on me. Nevertheless, Gerald himself, glancing around the tiny stage of the settlement music school and recalling his triumphant production of *The Marriage of Figaro,* seemed in peculiarly high spirits.

"I'll compose a Kaddish," Gerald said. "I'll wear a black armband."

Kaddish and a black armband. The poor boy was terribly confused. Maybe he was thinking of President Roosevelt when President Roosevelt's mother died. But Gerald's mind wouldn't work that way, and also it was the Kaddish that was out of whack, not the black armband. I wasn't sure whether or not to humor him, how to comfort him. He asked me to write a paper for him for Freshman Composition, and for once I agreed. It was on the split personality of Lewis Carroll and came back with a C. "Oh, sure," Gerald said bitterly, "but if she knew the great Lois Ackerman really wrote it . . ." "Gerald, that's not true," I said, wondering if it were. I didn't mention Glenda Green and he didn't bring her up either. "Discretion is the better part of valor," Rosalie said with less than her usual verve. She hadn't been herself ever since her debut.

2

In belated recognition of Walter's formal separation from the Army, we gave him a big welcome-home party, inviting all the relatives who had been at the seder, including Josef, of course, Gerald, who ate like family and tee-heed a lot out of embarrassment, Walter's best Army buddy, a fat jolly Italian who was still in uniform, a couple of Walter's prewar pals who had been mustered out of the service several months before, and Maria, whom Walter had asked me to invite and who smiled icily at the jolly Italian. The next night Walter and I went out on one of our dates, to a nightclub on Fourteenth Street called the Russian Kretchma, where we danced and laughed at the time I thought the food there was kosher, and the next day he slept until three and the day after that. By the end of the week it no longer seemed like a case of utter exhaustion. When he finally got up he went to Barney's and bought himself a new suit. It was a three-piece brown pepper-and-salt tweed with a vest that bulged a bit between the buttons. There was another suit almost exactly like it in mothballs in Walter's closet. The funny thing was that though it was Walter's room with Walter's things in it, his books, clothes, typewriter, clarinet, easel and oil paints, it still seemed to belong to Josef, more so than when Josef was in it. The other funny thing, though I didn't want to think about it, was that *Walter* was the one who was nice to Josef, Walter who took him to art galleries and chamber music concerts at Washington Irving High School on Saturday nights. He was still very much interested in Maria, but Maria wasn't having any, except to let him sit in on Sidney Hook's philosophy course with her down at the New School. Ultimately, Walter gave up on both her and Sidney Hook, and started going around with a terribly pretty, terribly stupid young refugee girl with an English-German accent, who looked like early pictures of our mother. My father took an instant dislike to her. I didn't understand it. True, Lisel really was stupid beyond belief. She would tell us, laughing, how when she was a schoolgirl in Vienna her father used to give her a gold charm for her bracelet every time she passed a test, and there were very few charms on that bracelet. But she was so good-natured about it all—she didn't even mind repeating "Brrussels sprrouts" for me so that I could marvel at the gutturals. And when you considered what she had been through.

"I mean, Daddy, she had to leave Vienna all alone

when she was ten. She was on a children's transport to London. They took her father away. She never saw her father again."

"Do you need any money?" my father said.

"No."

Good old Manny Ackerman. Why had I imagined he would be any different when I remembered how he had acted with Josef? He offered Walter money too, "to show the girl a good time," he said with a sour smile, and to my amazement Walter nodded sheepishly and accepted. As the relationship with Lisel turned "serious" my father even gave her money direct, with Walter's tacit acquiescence, for new clothes, once specifically for new underwear, and to my continued amazement, they took that too. Ultimately he also shelled out for a diamond engagement ring, wholesale naturally and bigger than Leonora's, but drew the line when Lisel began suggesting a Persian-lamb coat like mine. I wondered when Walter was going to draw the line too, but it was being an unexpectedly hard time for him, what with not wanting to go on to graduate school, though he was entitled to it on the GI Bill, and conversely not being able to find work that suited him either. He signed up for a couple of extension courses in journalism at NYU, but quit, then talked about being a *real* writer and started a novel, which he abandoned after three chapters. He decided maybe it would make a better play, but all the characters, men and women alike, sounded like the same person declaiming different portions of the same long monologue in turn, and it never got beyond Act I. It was like Odets, besides. Then he started writing letters to *Time,* sending them "kudos" for some article or other, on German militarism or the do-nothing Congress, but they didn't print any of them, and finally he even went down to their employment offices with a few specimens of his own version of Timese, only to come back reporting a runaround. "Forget it," my father said, "Luce doesn't hire Jews," and Walter agreed. "*Anti-semitn,* the whole empire," he said, lapsing into Yiddish, which he did increasingly lately and which kind of worried me. In fact, even his English seemed to be taking on a distinct Yiddish intonation and once in my presence a salesgirl at Woolworth's actually asked him sympathetically how long he had been here. "Really, Walter," I said, "you don't have to sound as if you just came over on the boat." Walter laughed. "*Anti-semitke,*" he said. But more and more Walter just hung around such places as Coney Island with his old Army cronies spending his days doing absolutely nothing, or else on the spur of the moment took Lisel and me to some Chinese or Mexican restaurant he had discovered in his wanderings—at my father's expense, I couldn't help thinking when Walter grabbed the check. He loved trying dishes nobody had ever heard of, and also crazy drinks. My friends and I from school drank crazy stuff too, but it seemed wrong in an older brother, downright disheartening, especially since Walter wouldn't stop once he got started, and went from singapore slings to boilermakers to god knew what else even after he had already turned green and bolted for the john several times. Lisel, contemplating her new engagement ring, remained remarkably impervious to what was going on —Should she really have chosen a white gold setting? Would yellow gold have better suited her skin tone? Were the baguettes too many or too few?—and just smiled at my brother affectionately each time he came lurching back to the table. I was terrified that he would pass out cold, and one night he finally did, in his own room, luckily, where I had dumped him on the studio couch, unhitching his arm after a terrible struggle down the hall. But Lisel didn't much mind that either, and cheerfully pulled on one trouser leg as instructed— I had seen it in *The Best Years of Our Lives*—while I pulled on the other. He was wearing khaki underwear and dog tags. I wondered if he had ever been rolled. Josef poked his head in the doorway, surveyed the scene, and smiled. I asked him to please leave, and so did Lisel, sharply, in German, without the please. She disliked Josef intensely and always asked why he had to hang around so much. But Josef only shook his head, removed Walter's pants expertly without a fumble, laughed and sat down with us. He laughed again when I quickly covered Walter with a blanket.

"Your brother took me to the Radio City Music Hall today," Lisel said, pointedly ignoring him.

"Really? Did you enjoy it?"

"Not the picture."

"*Great Expectations?*"

"I know the English too well to be taken in by them," Lisel said. "But the concert!"

"Oh? What did they play?" Was Walter at least breathing?

"Well, I don't remember the name of the piece or of the composer," Lisel said a trifle impatiently. "It was Charles Previn and his orchestra."

Walter opened one eye. In the silence, Lisel looked from one to the other of us.

"Don't you like music?" Lisel said.

3

"Don't I like music," I said. "For godssakes, I mean, really. And she knows the English too well to be taken in by *Great Expectations*. What the hell does that mean?"

Still, it was an incredibly beautiful May day. Behind Rosalie and me the apple orchard of the agricultural high school was fragrant and flowering. Strains of the *Liebestod* wafted toward us out of the open windows of Professor Curtis' classroom with every sweet breeze. We were even in our favorite spot on the softball field, the outer edges of center field where hardly anyone ever hit a ball and you could hang around and enjoy an hour's decent conversation. But Rosalie just stood there like a lump, fielder's mitt under her arm. She was wearing a green gym suit, which made her look fat, her mother's long rhinestone earrings, silk stockings and sneakers, all of which made her "out of uniform," as our phys. ed. instructor had put it, warning her for the last time. But none of it touched her.

She was in a private winter of her own. I couldn't believe that the nightclub fiasco had so crushed her spirit.
Where was her old flame, her spark? There would be
other auditions, people besides Luke to write her new
material. But this was what Rosalie should have said to
me, not vice versa. Also, for what it was worth, I
missed her, missed her more acutely than if she had
been physically absent, not that this news would have
touched her either.

"Walter's definitely going to marry her," I continued
anyway, wondering if maybe Leonora would think the
Music Hall story was funny. But that would have
meant telling her in front of Maria, and I didn't want
to do that. They didn't sit at the regular table in the
cafeteria anymore, but at a separate one in a corner
where they laughed in our direction. A recognized two-
some. When they walked on campus they went arm in
arm. Maria had taken to wearing a large cross. "In fact,
Lisel is planning a late June wedding. She read in a
magazine that June is the month for brides. My parents
are having a joint heart attack. They don't want little
Walter to get married so soon. Their sonny boy. Isn't it
ironic? They didn't worry like this when he was in the
Army. And also, when you think that all *I'm* supposed
to do is get married, that no other destiny for me
counts . . ."

Rosalie smiled patiently, which was a lot worse than
no smile. These days, I had begun to question the very
basis of our relationship. After all, even by her standards, wasn't empathy a two-way street? And I had listened to *her* problems, hadn't I, even when I hardly

knew her? Stuck around, cheered her through her Christmas doldrums, slept over on demand, placated her mother even when my heart wasn't in it? But now, when it was a question of *my* feelings, *my* parents, *my* brother . . . Also damn it, it was spring! Couldn't she smell the air, hear the music? "*Whan that Aprille with his shoures soote the droghte of March hath perced to the roote, and bathed every veyne in swich licour . . .*" My season! She was supposed to help see me through it. We had a gentleman's agreement that she would. Reading Chaucer wasn't enough! Besides which, I had a lousy professor.

I looked at the diamond, which was very far away and populated with players. Our phys. ed. instructor barked out a command. There was a sharp crack of a bat, and lots of squealing. Girls in gym suits started to run around the bases. For the first time in my college career I wished I were running with them.

"You should get a load of my mother," I said, turning away from the scene. "She hasn't stopped crying since Walter got engaged. She says Lisel can't speak English. Can you imagine?"

Still no reaction, even to the word "mother," a bait the old Rosalie used to rise to like a carp.

"Listen," I said finally, "if you feel so lousy you should have said you had your period and skipped class."

Rosalie gave me a funny look which I couldn't interpret. It wasn't that hard after all. All you had to do was mumble embarrassedly about strenuous exercise and it being *that* time of the month, and our phys. ed. instructor would nod abruptly and put a tiny check after your name, even if, as in the case of Rosalie, the checks were piling up to practically hemorrhage proportions. He was a nice guy, really, except for trying to drill us before each class. But that wasn't his fault. He had been a drill sergeant in the Army, and couldn't help trying to line us up, telling us to right-face, left-face, about-face, march two three four, hup two three four until we got all mixed up, bumping into each other, facing the wrong way, sometimes just marching off the field completely. The hell with it. I took a breath of the sweet air, and lifted my face to the sun.

"Oh, god, what a day for love," I said. "Don't you feel it?"

"What's it like to come?" Rosalie said quietly, staring off at the pitcher's mound.

I looked at her. "Have you never?"

"I don't think so."

"Well, it's a whole other thing. You'd know it."

Now that the ice was broken I wanted to say more, that—but suddenly the squealing was directed at us. We looked around with more than a little irritation. Somebody seemed to have hit a ball into the outfield and it had rolled into the grass near our feet. With an air of much-tried good nature, Rosalie stooped and threw the ball back. More squealing, more girls running around bases. Yolanda Ruhtz, one of our more athletic types, with buck teeth, black bushy hair, and ankle sneakers, marched grimly toward us as if she were paying a visit, and then picked up the ball from the bushes where it had landed a yard or so away. She didn't bother to throw it back to the pitcher so evidently the hour was over. Whether the game was over too was another matter. Whenever the time was up, everybody automatically stopped playing. I wasn't even sure if our side, whichever that was, had lost. Maybe we had been in the middle of a ninth-inning rally or some such. That was another thing, like our failure at drilling, that our phys. ed. instructor never got through his head. Each time it happened, he just kept blowing his whistle until he was red in the face. But now as usual all the girls started wandering off the field, whistle notwithstanding, and Rosalie and I wandered off with them. In the locker room, we calmly ignored Yolanda's dirty looks. Yolanda was king on the field but not here. Here she was just a homely girl overendowed with team spirit. When she took off her gym bloomers her pubic hair, as bushy as the hair on her head, made a big mound under her white cotton underpants. We waited out several more dirty looks and furious attempts to speak, and finally she left. Rosalie was wearing my old/new black lace underwear. The bra was too small and made her look like she had two sets of bosoms, one inside the bra, and one above it. I couldn't believe I had ever gone out and bought such scandalous stuff, but that was the kind of influence Rosalie used to have over me. I finished opening her combination lock for her and threw the door open.

"Rosalie," I said. "Empathy is a two-way street."

"Hm?"

"Empathy—"

"Oh, god," Rosalie said. "I don't want you to empathize with me this time."

"No?" I said coldly, more hurt than I let on. "How come?"

"Because you'd only throw up. What's your financial situation?"

I told her I had five hundred dollars in Defense bonds, not fully matured, and some Victory stamps. "Why?"

"I'm pregnant," Rosalie said.

Pregnant? *Rosalie?* But she had already clanged her locker door shut and, looking at me almost with pity, wandered off into a world where she knew I couldn't follow.

4

In a daze, I went over to the music room. Sherwin Schiff was prancing around as usual, and Gerald was picking out a score over at the piano. A familiar scene, except that I couldn't make anything of it. Also, Gerald was really in peculiarly high spirits, considering the fact of his mother. The thought of her and the word "doom" temporarily blotted Rosalie from my mind. It was as if Mrs. Muster were a black cloud hanging over Gerald's head. I couldn't think of anything else when I saw him these days. Maybe Gerald couldn't think of anything else either, but he was so blithe about it. In addition to his Kaddish, to be performed immediately after his mother's death, he was also deep in long-range plans for an English version of *Madame Butterfly*, which he meant to produce independently here at Medaglia. *An L. Gerald Muster Production*. He was obsessed with Gian Carlo Menotti's recent success and the whole matter of opera in English in general, and in fact was already designing the program. "I long to be rid of this ponderous obi," Gerald sang, taking Butterfly's part. "What do you think?" "It loses something in the translation," I said, deciding, no, it wasn't the right time to mention Rosalie. Not that Gerald would have minded, he loved scandal and juicy tidbits of all kinds.

With a funny look on his face, Gerald took some snapshots out of his wallet and handed them to me. With an even funnier look, Sherwin embraced me with less than his usual passionate quota of "Darlings!" and quickly sashayed out the door.

"I took them in the hospital," Gerald said proudly, almost gleefully. He waited for my reaction.

The snapshots were of his mother. She was sitting in a hospital chair, wearing a frilly negligee and staring into the camera with the bony depth and horror of an Auschwitz victim. How could he have taken them? How could she have permitted them to be taken? I handed them back, and he looked at them once more, smiling, before he replaced them in his wallet. The room was terribly dark after the beautiful spring light outside, but Gerald was talking about his Kaddish again, and I knew there was no way of luring him into the sunshine.

"*Yiskadal, v'yiskadash, shmai raboh,*" Gerald sang, tootling around on the keyboard, stopping to make a few notations. Well, at least he wasn't doing his Kaddish in English. "I haven't told her about it yet. She doesn't want to die. She kept saying last night, 'Don't let me die, Gerald, don't let me die.'"

"Oh, Gerald."

But Gerald only went tee-hee in a vague kind of way. And then when the next person wandered in, which happened to be Milton Schwartz, took out the snapshots again. Milton looked at me over Gerald's head but didn't say anything when he handed them back. Why couldn't any of us think of the right thing to say?

"You want to hear what Mommy said to me last night?" Gerald asked Milton. "She said, 'Don't let me die, Gerald, don't let me die.'"

5

"Where was his father?" Dr. Hamburger asked, also shrouded in darkness.

"His father? What difference does that make? She was asking *Gerald* not to let her die."

"You can't ask that of anyone."

"But you can! You can! You *have* to be able to." Dr.

Hamburger looked at me thoughtfully. And all the time, though I didn't say it, I kept wondering crazily where the funeral would be. Was there a Forest Hills branch of Campbell's or some other gentile establishment? What would my father say when he saw the announcement in the newspapers? Would he ask me if I had known all the time? If only Rosalie were around to consult. But she was all enmeshed in the intricacies of her own fate. Her boyfriend had come up with the name of some shady doctor in Union City and was making arrangements. I was relieved but also surprised. Somehow I had assumed that foolishly, quixotically, Rosalie would insist on having the baby. I had even marshaled all sane arguments against it. But when we spoke it was always about money. She refused to let Sam pay for "it"—we never said what—refused even to let him come with her. Sam agreed that it was wiser. It had something to do with his wife's private detectives and the legal separation, which hadn't deterred him from taking Rosalie to the Algonquin, I thought, though I didn't say so. I cashed in my Defense bonds, hoping that somebody in the bank would say I was too young, hoping that at the last minute Rosalie, my old Rosalie, would refuse to touch the proceeds. I most of all wanted to talk it over with Walter, a man of the world. But there was no use broaching the matter of sex to him, since he was so touchy on the subject, at least when it came to me. Once, for example, when he was still in the Army and it all lay heavily on my mind, I had written to him about just the possibility of theoretically losing my virginity one day, and he had shot me back a six page V-mail letter saying theoretically absolutely not. The kid sister syndrome. But didn't he and Lisel sleep together, hard as it was to believe? If they did it certainly wasn't uppermost in Lisel's mind. She was far more concerned with buying her trousseau, jotting down tips from *Bride's Magazine*, spending money like water, still angling for a Persian-lamb coat like mine, deliberating over the guest list though it consisted mainly of our friends and relatives, she and her mother having very few of their own. Now that it was coming so close, my parents were more and more depressed, pointing out other marriage possibilities to Walter, like my father's partner's daughter, who sat around the lobbies of Miami Beach hotels in her three-quarter ranch mink, waiting for Mr. Right to come along. "Think it over, boychick," my father kept saying. "Don't plunge into anything. You don't want it to be the Army all over again." My mother kept making him baked apples because he had once said he liked them. I unpinned Walter's infantry badge from the sweater where I had worn it ever since he went into the Army, unable to decide whether I wanted Walter to get married or not. I had always longed for a sister, but Lisel wasn't it.

Late one night, Rosalie came through with one of her urgent phone calls. She was in a booth in a candy store on the Grand Concourse. It was all set in Union City. I was to meet her on the subway platform the next morning at 8 A.M. sharp, cash in hand. I was there early, like a diplomatic courier, money stashed away in my briefcase between the *Complete Works of Chaucer* and Plato's *Dialogues,* looking around as if I had never seen a subway station before. Poor Rosalie. My heart ached for her until I realized that as usual she was going to be late. I still had these crazy notions about the baby. That we could adopt it communally, take care of it, bring it to the cafeteria. But even on this, the worst day of her life, my life, she couldn't manage to be on time. Possibly she would arrive wearing an eyepatch, two eyepatches. I bought a candy bar and a newspaper—Russia had violated her pledges to Austria, Truman's mother was still holding her own. Why did I think the world would change?—and peered down the length of the track for a moving light at the end of the tunnel. A train swept in, swept out, but Rosalie wasn't on it. Then a voice behind me said grimly: "It's all right. You can stop looking."

I wheeled around. *"Mrs. Golden."*

"It's all right," she repeated.

I stammered something about what a coincidence, and she smiled at me like death.

"You don't think I know why you're here?"

We both looked down at my briefcase.

"Keep your charity," Mrs. Golden said. "We're not charity cases."

"Oh, Mrs. Golden, I—"

It was awful, but suddenly at this worst possible moment all I could remember was a dopey story Rosalie had once told me about a family expedition to Coney Island when her father was alive. He was a garment cutter and he loved to chew gum. Mrs. Golden was always after him to spit it out. He refused, laughing at her exaggerated delicacy. "Go, children," she had said to them finally, "go into the next car. This is not for your eyes." Maybe I had smiled.

"You think it's funny?" Mrs. Golden said.

"Oh, no, I—"

"What is it with you children that to you life is only a game, your plaything? You see your parents worrying, crying, sacrificing, but it makes no impression. How is that? All you know is how to fool around like fools."

It wasn't fair. I was the dependable one, the sensible one, remember? The one she came to when she needed help with Rosalie? I felt the way I used to in class when the teacher punished all of us just because one student had misbehaved. And then I thought of Gerald passing around his ghoulish snapshots of his mother, then fiddling at the piano, and that neither Milton nor I, his staunchest friends, could think of a single way to help him through his darkest hour. I even noticed that Mrs. Golden wasn't wearing one of her usual dramatic costumes, but a simple neat navy blue spring coat and a flowered head scarf, with a pocketbook in one hand and a shopping bag in the other.

"Wait," Mrs. Golden said. "Someday you'll see."

"I have to go to school," I said.

Mrs. Golden nodded, as if I had insulted her again. "Definitely. Go. Anyway, it's done."

Done? "How is . . . she?"

"Hemorrhaging. She's in the hospital."

"Oh, my god."

"Don't worry about her. She'll be all right, our Rosalie. Only, now it's on her record. It will follow her all the rest of her life. What did she think, that they would believe her about the coat hanger? Does she think they're all fools?"

"Can I see her?"

"See her?" Mrs. Golden smiled bitterly, the way she used to smile at Rosalie's grand piano. "Do me a favor, my dear. Stay away from her. You and the rest of her fine 'friends.'"

I wanted to tell her that it wasn't fair to lump me with the others, that I *had* been Rosalie's friend, without any quotation marks.

"Or maybe I should thank you," Mrs. Golden said. "Maybe you'll tell me you meant well."

Oh, I did, I did. On the verge of tears, I wanted to tell her all my hopes and dreams for the baby, but already they sounded absurd. In any case, she so clearly wanted to get rid of me forever, that I felt almost as humiliated as she did. The next train to Queens came roaring in and I got on it quickly without looking back, wishing that a thief would rob me of my five hundred dollars, blood money, and didn't even glance out the window as we went rushing past 67th Avenue to see if Gerald were waiting for me on the platform, so far away did he seem. Of course, I might be pregnant too, a possibility that thrilled and terrified me every month, but that didn't seem very real now either.

The regular table in the cafeteria was deserted. Not even Maria and Leonora were around to laugh at us from a distance. Perhaps they were down in the Village, where Leonora had taken to reading her poetry in people's apartments. Or perhaps Leonora had cracked up again. The last thing Maria had told me, when she was still speaking to the world at large, was that Leonora's first breakdown had occurred when she was in Gorham—"the little illness" that Mrs. Edleman smilingly alluded to and what had brought her home to Medaglia—and that that time they had found her glued to a carousel horse. What made Leonora so equestrian in her madness? I wondered. Anyway, it was too late for breakfast, too early for lunch. I decided I couldn't face any classes and started my dreary way home again on the subway. I took out my *Complete Works of Chaucer*. I was supposed to do a special credit report on the mormal on the Cook's shin, but couldn't face that either. Whatever I had once felt about Chaucer, thanks to Dr. Ryder all the springtime had gone out of him. I put the volume back in my briefcase and opened Plato's *Dialogues* instead. I was no good at philosophy, or chess either, it turned out, but there was something about these *Dialogues* that got to me. I smoothed out a clean page of my notebook: "Aspects of Philos., pp. 98–99, May 27, 1947," and sighed. Oh, Rosalie, Rosalie, where are you? Why aren't you here? Please don't die.

"Perhaps you think I am braving you in what I am saying now, as in what I said before about the tears and prayers. But this is not so. I speak rather because I am convinced that I never intentionally wronged anyone. . . . THE UNEXAMINED LIFE IS NOT WORTH LIVING!"

Rosalie, please don't die.

Further down: "*I would rather die having spoken after my manner, than speak in your manner and live.*"

Lower down: "*And I prophesy to you who are my murderers, that immediately after my departure punishment far heavier than you have inflicted on me will surely await you. Me you have killed because you wanted to escape the accuser, and not to give an account of your lives. But that will not be as you suppose; far otherwise. For I say that there will be more accusers of you than there are now. . . . If you think that by killing men you can prevent them from censuring your evil lives, you are mistaken.*"

The knowledge of absolutes before birth. Forgetting absolutes after birth. Learning is simply recollection. Cebes to Socrates: "*There is a child within us to whom death is a sort of hobgoblin: Him too we must persuade not to be afraid when he is alone in the dark.*"

Did Rosalie's baby know the absolutes? Would he have forgotten them already? Then be forced to start relearning what he had been born knowing? Was he alone in the dark?

Bot. page: "*. . . And hitherto most of us had been able to control our sorrow; but now when we saw him drinking, and saw too that he had finished the draught, we could no longer forbear, and in spite of myself my own tears were flowing fast; so that I covered my face and wept, not for him, but at the thought of my own calamity in having to part from such a friend.*" His legs grow cold and then upwards and upwards. Says, "*Crito I owe a cock to Asclepius; will you remember to pay* *the debt?" "The debt shall be paid," said Crito, "is there anything else?"* No answer. *"Such was the end, Echerates, of our friend; concerning whom I may truly say, that of all men of his time whom I have known, he was the wisest and the justest and best."*

I got off the subway train at the next stop and threw up.

6

It turned out to be the flu. I spent a week in bed taking sulfa and drinking grapefruit juice. My mother kept shaking her head over me and suggesting an enema. Walter brought me *Newsweek*, which he had now switched to as more liberal than *Time*, though it was thinner and a lot less interesting. He had decided to buy *Time* only when they ran the current events quiz and urged me to take it with him, knowing he would do better, especially on the maps. I leafed through an article by J. Edgar Hoover telling how to fight Communism, and put it down when my mother said I would go blind. "Brrussels sprrouts," Lisel said to cheer me up. "Brrussels sprrouts." Gerald called and said he had found a divine little pillbox for me on Third Avenue. I didn't ask him what he was doing on Third Avenue though I had an idea. I took some more sulfa. The new wonder drug. Nothing was too good for Manny Ackerman's daughter. At night I heard him and Walter quarreling. Walter talked of going to Mexico, which now that Truman and Alemán had exchanged visits seemed to appeal to him. I wanted to go too. As if he knew this, my father bought me pink sweetheart roses and baby's breath, which suggested funerals and lovers at the same time. Would he have bought me pink sweetheart roses and baby's breath if he knew I wasn't a virgin? Something not to discuss with Dr. Hamburger.

7

"Spring cold or spring fever?" Dr. Lorillard said cheerfully, beckoning me into her office from the hall where I had been standing reading some notices I had already read a thousand times. Mainly applications for summer school. Oneonta College was offering a course on the UN, Claremont a program for "those seriously interested in creative writing: poetic, narrative, and expository." *Summer.* Where would we all be? Gerald spoke of two weeks in Tanglewood, without me. I could picture him lying on a blanket with a male/female *someone* listening to the Boston Symphony in the hot velvet summer night. Milton and Ruthie would be home in Forest Hills with her parents and the new baby, which was due any day now. They were still very cheerful, unaware that fate was closing in on them in the worst way. I couldn't get any clear picture of Rosalie or of me. For me maybe Lewisohn Stadium with Robert, sitting side by side on hard stone steps and rented pillows. I hadn't called Rosalie at home because I didn't want to get her mother by mistake. I hadn't tried to reach her at Sam's because I didn't want to get Sam by mistake.

"It was only a cold," I said, entering Dr. Lorillard's office reluctantly. Well, at least Slavitt wasn't there, though as usual his empty desk was accusation enough. Of what? What was he always accusing me of, come to think of it? What did he want of me, anyway?

"We missed you in class," Dr. Lorillard said.

"Thank you. Actually, it was the grippe."

"Our loss, our loss. You always have so much to contribute."

I thanked her again. She reached down into her drawer for her capacious teacher's pocketbook, and looked up smiling her broad ladylike gap-toothed smile.

"Do you think you'll be well enough by next Saturday to come to a party?" Dr. Lorillard said mischievously.

"A party?"

"At Dr. Slavitt's house."

"Dr. Slavitt?"

Was it only the fact of Dr. Lorillard's being a lady that made us echo each other endlessly, in a version of John's well-bred Yale stammer, or was it something more? Something worse, something deeper?

"We try to rotate the annual department get-together."

"The annual department party? But I don't belong there."

"You do, you do," Dr. Lorillard said, blurting out her laugh. "Our prizewinner. Prizewinner."

"I've won a prize?" I said warily.

"For the best essay. It won't be announced until graduation. But there's no need to keep it a secret from *you,* is there? Considering your tact and discretion. Discretion."

I closed my eyes briefly, whether from despair or sudden physical debility I wasn't sure. In any case, there was no need for her to tell me what effort of mine, as she would have put it, had established me as a Medaglia prizewinner. *The Humor of Character in Charles Lamb's Essays of Elia,* what else? Was I to be haunted by the thing forever? It was a distinct possibility. Evidently, as she explained it, there were even plans afoot to mimeograph it for use in the teaching of Freshman Composition. A model research paper, though I would be required to use a pseudonym, of course. Of course. With positive pleasure. My god, suppose Gerald failed Freshman Comp. again and had to read it for homework?

"I guess we can show these Slavitts a thing or two," Dr. Lorillard said with another blurted laugh.

"Slavitts. A thing or two," I agreed, and headed for the smokestacks of the cafeteria, trying not to think of what smokestacks reminded me of these days. These days.

8

For all his hauteur and intellectual grandeur, Dr. Slavitt lived in Sunnyside in a gray-brick semi-detached two-family house. In spite of what Dr. Lorillard had said about my being invited on account of the essay prize, which I hadn't mentioned to anyone, least of all Gerald, it turned out that I wasn't the only student present, which was a relief and also a curious disappointment. Leonora was there too, in honor of her Proust in the original, I supposed, and also Marcel Mandelbaum, who walked around showing the fruits of his latest bout with the Muse on the GG to anybody who was willing to read them, which included several department husbands and wives, who were looking trapped anyway. Leonora and Marcel, Slavitt's pets, so he must have had a hand in the guest list, though when Robby Wilson arrived, Houghton's boy, I amended this to teacher's pets in general. The little living room grew surprisingly and unfamiliarly crowded what with the faculty mates I had never seen before, and in a certain sense ought not to have existed. Though of course the chief guest, our permanent department guest of honor, so to speak, was our Walt Whitman scholar, who occupied the same wing chair the whole time, as dignified and immobile as he was in his always open and empty office, complete with pince-nez and Herbert Hoover collar. He was the only one who looked the same as he did in school. The other members of the faculty seemed strange and uncomfortable even to themselves, what with their dressy clothes and drinks and party smiles and postures and party chatter. Particularly the party chatter, when in class they usually said everything slowly, twice, and waited by the blackboard to have notes taken on it. They were even more out of their element than Marcel and Leonora and Robby and I, who stood together in a mute uneasy cluster, like Laocoön and his stony sons, breaking apart to make a brief foray here and there, before we regrouped again. My own little excursion was to sally forth to the buffet table where Dr. Lorillard, in a beige brocade cocktail dress which consorted oddly with her boyish bob and gap-toothed smile, was drinking Slavitt's ready-made manhattans. "Our prizewinner!" she cried each time in an ever louder voice, "prizewinner!" blurting out that laugh, while Leonora looked on with a supercilious smile. Then, for no reason, I would go upstairs to where the coats were piled on the bed, sigh, and sit down and powder my nose. It got to be practically a reflex. I thought that maybe subconsciously I associated compacts with scholarship on account of Dr. Lorillard and her preparations for her seminar. A few times while I sat on the bed, people emerged from the bathroom, once the Walt Whitman specialist buttoning his fly, another time Mrs. Slavitt, who proved to be quite pleasant and motherly-looking in her navy blue dress. I went downstairs again for what I definitely decided would be my last time and ran right into Dr.

Lorillard who once again proclaimed me our prize-winner.

"Don't sell out," Dr. Houghton said, who was even drunker than she was. "Whatever you do, don't sell out."

"Oh, she won't," Dr. Lorillard assured him. "She's the finest student I've ever had. Except one."

"Who was that?"

"Leonora Edleman."

I looked at her uncomprehending and as if for the last time, and turning away encountered Dr. Geoffrey, monkey-faced and complete with husband, talking about the pure snows of Austria to Mrs. Slavitt and, with a helpless very sophisticated laugh, of the lack of café life in America. They had been in the neighborhood and as soon as she finished her glass of white wine—another helpless laugh—were going to give Dr. Lorillard a ride back to Manhattan. I thought of cadging a lift too and decided against it. It made me very nervous to see her and Allan these days, and had ever since Gerald told me the latest piece of juicy gossip: that Dr. Geoffrey had been having an affair with the young man Quentin, which I had suspected, and that her husband was too, which I hadn't suspected. She had found them both in bed together. In Allan's room, the one that faced the street? I kept getting different pictures of it in my mind. Did she cry, throw things, pull a tantrum, slink off to one of her bistros and get drunk? All I saw clearly was two tousled male heads emerging above the sheets.

"And how are you, my dear?" Dr. Geoffrey said.

"Fine, thanks."

"Really fine?" Dr. Geoffrey said with a sad wise Austrian smile. "Or are you just saying that?"

I went upstairs again. Yes, it was certainly time to leave. The question was merely how. It wasn't so easy to dismiss yourself from a group of people who generally dismissed you. I sat down on the bed again, considering my getaway (had she really said Leonora *Edleman?*), and this time Dr. Slavitt himself emerged from the bathroom.

"Leaving so soon?" he said, making it into a kind of challenge.

"It's time, isn't it?"

"Hurry up please, it's time," he said sardonically.

"The Wasteland," I said, "so what?" emboldened by the fact that the term was almost over and that though we were in his house we weren't in his class, and I wasn't ever going to take any more of his courses anyway. Actually, most of what I had learned this year was from Dr. Lorillard and that was mainly about martinis and avocados and not taking praise too much to heart. *He* could give me any mark he wanted.

"Wait a minute," Dr. Slavitt said. "I want to talk to you."

"Look, Slavitt," I said, "if it's about that paper I think it stinks too. In fact, I hate Charles Lamb. I love Alexander Pope!"

"I'm concerned about your intellectual development."

"I still love Pope. And I hate your precious Whitman. All he does is talk about himself. And I had nothing to do with that prize."

"For godssake you need broadening. You don't *know* anything."

"I am quite aware," I said coldly, putting away my compact and rising, "that that is your opinion."

"You don't know my opinion of anything either," Dr. Slavitt said. "I want you to go to Europe. France. England. Expose yourself to a real cultural tradition. Not these spider droppings at Medaglia."

I was fed up with spider droppings too. But *Europe?* I had taken three years of French. Two years of Latin in high school. But the idea of Europe in terms of my own self-expression was astonishing. All I could think of was refugees. Steerage. Reconstruction work. In my confusion I took out my compact again.

"Put that goddamn thing away," Dr. Slavitt said.

"Listen, why are you always picking on *me?*" I said. "What do you want from *me?* Why do you ask *me* questions about the *Areopagitica* at nine A.M. in the morning?"

"Someday, god forbid, you may have to teach," Dr. Slavitt said. "But meanwhile, do you know what it's like at nine A.M. in the morning, as you put it, to see an intelligent face like yours? Can you imagine what it's like in the midst of those culture hounds and yahoos to see you at nine A.M.?"

"*Me?*" What about Leonora and Marcel Mandelbaum, and all the rest of them who knew what he was saying?

In the midst of my confusion, he had gripped me by

the shoulders and was pointing me towards the mirror over the bureau. In the midst of my confusion, he was turning me around again and kissing me. Passionately. In his own bedroom. His wife's bedroom. We broke apart. I stared at him, so tired and old, so intellectual, maybe even a card-carrying Communist, all of which seemed to amount to the same thing. Had he kissed me because I was such a good student or admired my mind in spite of everything, or what?

"But I thought you hated me," I said.

"Hated you?" Dr. Slavitt asked.

"I mean on account of the New Criticism and everything."

9

It was bad enough that Milton's baby was born premature. ("Premature," my father said.) But on top of that they had a *bris* for him and everything. I couldn't help feeling that Dr. Slavitt would disapprove, though it wasn't his business. Gerald and I drove out to Forest Hills in his father's car, stiff and starched as an aunt and uncle, but there were plenty of real aunts and uncles there already. I recognized them from the wedding. Plus herring and schnapps and dry cakes. Gerald and I hung around not quite knowing what to do with ourselves, put off by Milton and Ruthie's good-humored laughter, and smell of baby talc that failed to mask another smell we didn't want to think about. We had both chipped in to buy a silver rattle from Tiffany's, but they had unwrapped it the same as the other presents and laughed over it the same way, without being the least impressed by its elegance. They also teased poor Myrna, who didn't seem to mind a bit. The rabbi, also left over from the wedding, and his sidekicks got through doing whatever they had to do to the poor baby and we all crowded in to see him. There wasn't much to see, just a tiny squalling bundle of humanity in a vast expanse of crib. His name was Arnie, a ridiculous name, and Milton looked ridiculous holding him. A proud beaming young father, except that he didn't look like any father I had ever seen. The baby's crib was in their bedroom, but that didn't bother Milton and Ruthie either. They doted on the infant, even what he deposited in his diapers. "Mustard," Milton said, beaming harder, "he makes mustard." It was disgusting. Milton had begun not to look like any artist I had ever seen either. I was glad when some boisterous relatives called him into another room for a *"l'chaim."* I was even gladder Rosalie wasn't around to see all this. I had spoken to her on the phone a few times and she was much better physically, but worse emotionally. Suffering had definitely not ennobled her. All she could talk about, with great dramatic pauses and emphases, was the hospital and the emergency room and her copious bleeding. She laughed over her lie about the coat hanger as if that too were only another triumphant way of getting out of an exam. Her mother was there, however, looking grim as death, just as she had on the subway platform, except when she was warming up to the relatives. Also she was back in costume, the same black satin dress with the regal collar she had worn when I came to dinner. I wanted to feel for her but couldn't, she had been too mean to me. She avoided looking at me as if I were tainted. Suddenly I was alone in the bedroom. I looked around to make sure no one was watching.

"Tell me the absolutes," I whispered, bending over the crib. "Tell me the absolutes, Arnie."

"Go ahead," Ruthie said behind me. "Pick him up."

I backed away. Milton came in with Gerald. He thrust the baby into my unwilling and unwitting arms.

"You look good holding him," Milton said. "You look good."

I glanced embarrassedly at Gerald, who smiled at me fondly. A flush rose to my cheeks. I thought of my mother and felt sick. "Is this what you want?" Dr. Slavitt's voice murmured in my ear. "Is this what you want?" I thrust the baby back at Milton. Go away, Slavitt. I didn't want to think of him. Whenever I did I felt shaky and hot all over. I was determined to avoid him at all costs, and yet at the same time was desperately anxious that I would miss his class. In spite of myself I kept reenacting that kiss whenever I was alone, particularly in bed at night, when all the sweet juices started rising. He treated me the same as ever in class, with his usual icy irony, but he looked at me peculiarly. Or so I thought. Yes, our eyes *met*. What had ever made me imagine that tiny Arnie, busy making his mustard, had ever known the absolutes? "Darling, let's get out of here," I whispered to Gerald, detaching him from a group. "Mrs. Muster," he murmured back, grinning idiotically. On the way to the subway he cozied up to me in his father's car, and when we came to the station kissed me with a look in his eye I didn't want to see there.

"What are you thinking?" he said.

"About the Algonquin."

"I have to go see Mommy in the hospital!" Gerald cried, snapping out of it.

I descended the subway stairs feeling we had all aged a great deal lately. For some reason, I put my encounter with Dr. Slavitt into this category.

10

Actually, the person I really wanted to see was Walter. I missed our strange dates and midnight conversations more than I had expected to. A lost dimension in my life. But Walter was worn and haggard. He hadn't shaved in several days and looked as if he were sitting shiva. There were no more trips to Coney Island with his cronies, no more discovering of exotic restaurants. He emerged only for meals, and then went back to his room where he had again taken to sleeping until three o'clock in the afternoon. Sometimes I heard the sound of a clarinet, in imitation of Artie Shaw, sometimes I smelled oil paints, but I never saw him playing and never saw a painting. With his good-humored consent my mother began to swipe little bits of clay from his room, which she fashioned into tiny tea sets, complete with cups and saucers. This made her as proud and happy as a child, as if Walter's stuff had been put to good use after all. For the hell of it, I tried making a spoon or two, which were too large, and that made my mother happy also. It gave her an edge over me, and she immediately started to reduce them.

That Sunday, when I came home from the bris, Walter's door was still forbiddingly closed. I went to my room to think my life over, try to put it on a plane that I could understand or at least accept. But the sweet sick smell of baby talc lingered in my nostrils, reminding me of a very unacceptable future. My mother poked her head in the doorway, sniffing too, and then without invitation took a few steps inside. Almost automatically, she ran a finger over my desk, exploring for dust, and then took one of my father's handkerchiefs from her apron pocket and wiped the windowsill. I hated to see her use his handkerchiefs this way. She looked out the window for a moment— my mother was a great one for looking out windows and always prided herself on having an apartment in the front—then turned around, blowing her nose.

"Why are you crying?" I said. "I'm not doing homework."

"Who's crying? I have sinus. So how was the bris? You weren't jealous?"

"Mama, please leave me alone."

She didn't budge. "He won't eat. He's going to Argentina. Will the food there be any better?"

"Mexico." She still didn't budge. "Well, what do you want me to do about it? Force-feed him?"

I tried to remember how fond I had been of her at Schrafft's, and failed. Who had invented mothers anyway? I was tired of the whole pack of them, Ruthie Schwartz included. Guilt machines. How had Ruthie permitted such a thing to happen to her?

"Is Lisel going with him?" I said.

"He wouldn't tell me."

"Then why are you telling *me*? What do you want *me* to do about it?" For of course she did want me to do something about it. That was why she had come moseying into my room now, when my father wasn't home and couldn't stop her.

"He listens to you," my mother said. "He believes in you."

"Walter? That's ridiculous. He's a grown-up man. He has a life of his own. Why don't you just let him live it?"

But she was shaking her head, obstinate. Once my mother had a thought, she clung to it like a spar in a shipwreck.

"And what would you like me to say? Walter, dear, Mama's crying. Break your engagement. Marry the girl in the three-quarter mink."

Silence.

"What have you got against poor Lisel anyway?"

"She's not educated. She doesn't know English."

"Do you? Do you even know where Mexico is?"

But my mother rode that one out too, a hulk crashing and rising again with each buffet of the waves.

"And how do you know his next girl would be better educated? Maybe dumb ones are his type. It's not an unusual male characteristic."

She busied herself wiping out a clean ashtray, picking up the blouse I had tossed aside before leaving for the bris, with a mind to take it to the hamper.

"No, I'm sorry," I said. "I have no intention of meddling in Walter's affairs. I'll leave that to you and Daddy."

My mother nodded and left the room, my blouse in hand, docile and uncomplaining, except that there was a glint of triumph in her eye.

I walked down the hall to Walter's room, with nothing in mind really, and no delusions of power or grandeur. It was just that I hadn't talked to him in a long time. Lisel and her Brussels sprouts were always in the way, and also I wanted to get the taste of that bris out of my mouth somehow. I knocked lightly and let myself in. I had expected Walter to look mournful or perhaps be deep asleep, but he was sitting in an armchair in a khaki shirt, absorbed in a book. It was about how to write successful radio plays.

"Video is really where it's at, though," Walter said, tapping on the cover. "Mark my words."

I didn't know why I was so disappointed. Had I really expected to cheer him up, change the course of his life? Kudos to CBS.

"Mama sent me," I laughed, sitting down on his studio couch. "She says you're not eating."

He turned a page.

"But I would have come anyhow."

He sighed and laid aside the book. Except for the dark stubble he looked very handsome.

"I'm back from a bris, believe it or not."

"At your age? In your circles?"

"Marriage and babies seem to be all the rage everywhere," I said. "God, I hope I never have any children. Do you?"

"Not particularly."

"Me neither. Well, children maybe, but not babies." I didn't ask what Lisel wanted. She was no longer relevant.

Still, I thought, looking at him, in one way my mother and father were right. *Something* in Walter's life had to be relevant. It couldn't all be a matter of unfinished novels and aborted romances. Even his Army career had been blighted. He had enlisted right after Pearl Harbor with much weeping and much fanfare, and even got sent overseas. But it was only to mop up after Patton's tanks, seeing practically no action, and when he came back they sent him off to help close up a replacement depot. I thought of Martin Edleman, the dashing Air Force officer, and immediately felt disloyal. But where was the glamour and excitement I had always expected of my own impressive older brother? The artist, the intellectual? "Listen, Lois," my father had said, "just thank God he wasn't killed," and of course he was right.

"Not that it's any of my business," I said casually, too casually. Walter gave me a wary look. "But what's up with you two? Is that wedding on or off?"

"Don't you have homework?" Walter said.

"I'll do it later. What's Mama crying about?"

"My wasted life. Look, kid—"

"Walter darling, don't say that about your life," I said. "Even as a joke. It's all before you."

"Sure," Walter said.

"No, really, no kidding. Don't close the books on it so soon. Though I suppose you will have to go through with it, the wedding, I mean."

"Why?"

"Because you have to go through with *something*."

Walter looked surprised rather than hurt. I had sounded condescending and awful, when I had only meant to show him I was on his side. I looked around his room as the Turkish students looked around the cafeteria. Three or four unfinished paintings were set to dry by the radiator. Portraits of Lisel. None of them were finished and none of them looked like her.

"I think you should call her," I said. "The poor girl probably doesn't understand any of this."

"And what do you suggest I say?"

"I don't know. Something about you need time to think things over. That there's no point committing yourselves to a course of action that will only make you both miserable. That it's better to find things out now than when it's too late. That sort of thing."

"Is Papa home?" Walter said.

"Not yet. Look," I said, "*I* don't want you to get

married either. I'm more convinced of that than ever. In fact . . . it would be nice in a way, you know?"

"What would be nice?"

I shrugged. "You know . . . the two of us together . . . kind of, well . . . like Charles and Mary Lamb."

Walter immersed himself in his radio plays again. "I keep forgetting how young you are," Walter said.

My mother was waiting expectantly by the door. "*Nu?*"

I gave her a dirty look and went back to my room to do some homework. Even writing a paper on the mormal on the Cook's shin was better than realizing what an ass I had just made of myself. After a while my father came home. I gathered that he had been out to see my cousin in Brooklyn, which was a strange thing for him to do on a Sunday, or any other day for that matter. Despite my many promises to myself I had never paid Josef a visit. My father looked glum. He had stopped at the synagogue and brought back a yahrzeit candle, which he lit and set on top of the television set before dinner. It was the anniversary of his mother's death and maybe that was what had affected him. It was hard to say. He never spoke much about his mother except to remark that she was a saint. We sat down to my mother's overcooked and underseasoned meat loaf, broccoli, and mashed potatoes, not mentioning Walter though we were all thinking of him. The maid, who wasn't around on Sundays, had never figured out whether he was now the one to please.

"So what did you do today, Lois?" my father said. "Did you get any fresh air?"

"She went to a bris," my mother said.

"That's nice."

"Really? Well, frankly I think it's a barbaric custom."

"When you get older, you'll find out barbaric customs are often meaningful," my father said, and looked up. "*Walter.*"

"Where are you going?" my mother said. "I made baked apples."

"I just came in to get some milk. I have to make a phone call," Walter said. He had changed into a white shirt and tie and he didn't look at me.

"Eat something more substantial," my father said. "The call can wait." Then: "Tell her she can keep the ring. It's okay. She'll get a nice little piece of change out of it. She earned it."

"Daddy—" I started to say. But Walter was nodding sheepishly and smiling. In fact, everybody was smiling except me.

"Thanks, guv'nor," Walter said, pulling up a chair to where his place was already set.

"How's Josef?" I said, to change the subject and because I was ashamed of us. "I haven't seen him in a long time."

My father and mother and Walter exchanged glances.

"Forget it," my father said.

"Why should I?"

"Because he's disappeared. Kaput."

"But, Daddy, surely someone knows—"

My father shrugged. "They say he went to Palestine."

Palestine? It was incredible. Another boat? Another tag? Would the man wash up on shore after shore forever?

"Who knows if he even belongs to us," my father said.

"Oh, *Daddy*."

"Hey, kid, how about a date Saturday night?" Walter said quickly, interrupting. Kid. A date Saturday night. It was like being pinned with his infantry badge all over again. And what would I tell Gerald?

"Okay," I finally said. "Sure. Why not?"

Then I was smiling too. Suddenly the radiator pipes began to clank. It had been a fickle spring, and for days on end our apartment had been freezing, our landlord's private protest against rent control. And now, on this hottest day of the year, steam began to hiss. What a landlord. We all laughed. Well, for the rest of the night our house would be warm.

11

The next morning I got to campus early. Walter was going to CBS, and my father told him to take it easy. It had started to drizzle, nothing serious, just weather to match my mood. Pathetic fallacy, as Dr. Houghton would have put it, who also encouraged us to take notes on "the other side of the tapestry," and not being able "to see the forest for the trees." I sneezed a few times and felt lonely. Well, at least the cafeteria would be warm, and maybe there would be somebody to talk to. I pushed open the big glass doors and at once I saw Rosalie. She was at the "secluded" table by the stairs, eating a piece of huckleberry pie, pursuing each crumb and crushed berry with the tines of her fork. I sat down next to her, but aside from a quick nod, she hardly acknowledged my presence. Except for the nod, I wouldn't have been sure she even recognized me.

"You're back," I said. "How do you feel?"

"How should I feel?"

"I meant physically."

"Excuse me," Rosalie said. She edged past me, walked over to the food counter, and returned with a large piece of chocolate layer cake, which she ate layer by layer, ignoring the fact of me waiting for her to say something. When she finally finished, she sat musing over the soiled plate. She was wearing a sweater I had never seen before. Black this time, with pairs of lips done in red sequins all over it. Where her forehead met her hair, little trickles of perspiration were turning her powder orange.

"Something happened," I said.

"Ah, but what?" she said in a flat voice not her own, like a person in a trance. "There's the rub."

"You don't know?"

"I wish I did, believe me. I've gone over it in my mind a hundred times." She looked at me and then away again, as if there were no hope there. "She wanted me to break up with Sam."

"Well, that figures." Rosalie looked at me again. "I mean from her point of view."

"Well, I told her I wasn't breaking up. I told her I was moving in with him, in fact."

Oh, god. "And she said?"

"The sooner the better."

That figured too, though I didn't say so.

"Also, she would finance no more abortions. For that I should go to my friends." We both cleared our throats. "And not to be surprised if he sold me into white slavery. You know, the usual."

"Sure."

Rosalie shrugged. "So then I went into my room to pack. I was waiting for her to come. I mean, she had to. It was in the cards. Only you should have seen her. My god, screaming like a wild woman, braids down to her nose. Also, she had something in her hand. She was pointing it at her heart and screaming, 'Stab me! Go ahead, stab me and get it over with!' So I got scared. And then I looked and all she was holding was this little tiny pencil. Clifton's, left over from his urine specimen deliveries. So I took it away from her, and she was crying and I was crying, and we're holding each other, and the next thing I know I'm still in the Bronx."

Rosalie gave me a long look. Her eyes went back and forth across my face as if she were trying to read my mind.

"Do you want anything?"

"No."

She stood up. The red sequins on her sweater twinkled all over. One pair of lips was smoking a cigarette.

"I don't know," Rosalie said. "I keep thinking, if it had been anything but a *pencil* . . ."

12

Gerald's mother died that evening. The funeral would take place the day after tomorrow. Tomorrow the notice would be in all the papers. There was no question of my going. Mrs. Muster had hated me like poison. I wasn't formally engaged to Gerald. I was in no sense of the word a relative. I supposed some of the other kids would turn up, sitting alongside each other as awkwardly and clumsily as we had at Milton's wedding. Yes, I could see Milton and Ruthie side by side, conservative married mourners, ready to report back if necessary. But I didn't want them to. It would have meant explaining why I hadn't gone also. My father asked if I would be attending services and I said no. He nodded approvingly, assuming I supposed that I was afraid of dead people, which I was. He felt that young people had no business with the dead anyway. This had come up before when I was in high school and all the fathers were dying. "If they're sitting shiva," my father said, "just bring them something sweet. A box of candy, some miniature Danish. Say you're sorry. That's all that's required. Sit for a while, join in the general conversation, politics is okay, then go. Don't be afraid to laugh. It's all right to laugh on such occasions." Oh, Daddy. What did he know about Episcopalians and black armbands? I felt sick to my stomach. My mother wanted me to take my temperature, and I explained to her about the aftereffects of sulfa, which she believed. In the morning, waiting for the subway train—I always expected to see Mrs. Golden among the passengers—I bought the *Times* at the newsstand, then the *Daily News*. "Josephine Muster, beloved wife of Norman, devoted mother of Gerald . . ." It was funny to see Gerald's name in print, probably he thought it was exciting. "Services at the Riverside Memorial Chapel . . ." The *Riverside?* How was that possible? I felt sick again, this time with relief, as if I had been snatched from the jaws of death myself. No L. for Laurence. This was odd too. Should I call Gerald? I had no idea how to handle this business of mourning. I didn't think Gerald did either. But there would surely be family to guide him along, older people, people used to baked funeral meats and burial breakfasts, or whatever Episcopalians did at such times. The only thing I still had to go on was when President Roosevelt's mother died.

The next night, Gerald called at the usual hour, a little after eleven, and chatted like a normal person. He even sang me more snatches of *Butterfly*. "Then the trim white vessel sa-ails into the harbor." He was home alone with his father. His grandmother had gone back to her own house.

"Was it okay?" I said finally.

"Was what okay?"

"The funeral."

"Sure."

I hesitated, then delicately brought up the matter of Riverside. "Funny, I mean odd, that she should have been buried from there."

"Why?"

"Because she isn't, wasn't, you're not Jewish."

"Darling, who said I wasn't Jewish?"

"You did."

"Oh, my god," Gerald said. "You didn't believe that, did you?"

He went tee-hee.

13

I found my father sitting in front of the television set in his pajamas, drinking a glass of ginger ale. The baseball game he had been watching was over and the station was signing off. An American flag rippled in the lonely stratosphere to the accompaniment of "The Star-Spangled Banner," and then there was a beep and a wavy test pattern.

"For this alone it's worth owning a set," my father said. "Those are some Yankees this season."

"I'm going to Europe," I said.

"What's in Europe?" my father asked, not particularly paying any attention. He leaned forward and fiddled with the dial. There was nothing else on.

"I'm concerned about my intellectual development. I want to expose myself to a real cultural tradition."

"That's nice. It's some cultural tradition," my father said.

"Well, I'm tired of the spider droppings at Medaglia."

"Spider droppings is what you're studying?"

"It's not all pogroms and steerage and concentration camps, you know."

"I'm glad to hear that."

"Oh, Daddy. Anyway, I didn't say *now*. I mean eventually."

"Good. Keep me posted."

He was still not paying attention. And why should he? I had never even asked him anything. I had never seen Russia. I didn't even know who won the ball game. Suddenly I wanted to tell him that I loved him, but I didn't know how to do that either. Or at least find out what was worrying him. Because he was worried about something, I could tell. Why else would he sit here watching test patterns so late at night? Not Walter and Lisel. That was over. She was keeping the ring, Walter and I had a date Saturday night. Maybe business? He never let me ask about it, but I could have insisted. Was Lowyse Frocks doing well or badly in this uncertain postwar economy? Was he having trouble with his partner? Was that why he wanted Walter to take out the daughter? Were they going to cut velvet? I had never asked about any of that.

He shut off the set. I remembered the yahrzeit candle flickering on top of it.

"Tell me about your mother," I said.

"My mother?" my father said smiling. "My mother was a mother."

"Yes, but I don't know anything about her really."

"You saw the picture, Lois."

"But that's only a picture. What was she like? How did she sound? What did she wear?"

"She wore a pair of diamond earrings," my father said with a short laugh.

"But I thought you were poor."

"Poor wasn't the word for it. The diamond earrings were left over from her dowry. But she had to hock them too when my father died. We had nothing to eat."

"You mean she went to a pawnbroker?"

"No, no," my father said. "She went to a rich aunt. It was the custom in those days to go to a relative when you needed a loan and leave a little something as collateral. It was a formality so you shouldn't be ashamed. And was that aunt rich, not only by shtetl standards. The woman had everything. I should only see such dough. Jewelry, furs, who knows what else. They lived in a big estate on top of a hill. They even had their own fire engine."

"Well, what happened?" I said, feeling almost as if I were talking to Rosalie.

"What happened was that for seven years we worked like dogs in the grocery store, just like in the Bible, and then we scraped up enough and went back up the hill. Clean, dressed in our Shabbos best. My mother was a proud woman. She taught us self-respect.

We didn't come begging, after all. Oh, such a proud look on that woman's face."

"She must have been so happy when she got her earrings back."

"What earrings? We begged and pleaded but the aunt said she didn't even know what we were talking about. We came back empty-handed." My father sighed. "All right? Enough family stories?"

"But, Daddy, what did you do?"

"What could I do? I came to America. I married your mother. I worked in a sweatshop, again like a dog. I brought over my brothers and sisters. My mother didn't want to come, she had no heart for a new life. Then came the revolution, then the war. She was stuck there."

"I think you should have just sent her another pair."

"One pair?" my father said, smiling ironically. "Never mind. What difference does it make? A wonderful woman, a saint."

"I hope the aunt died."

"She did."

"And her children?"

"They said they didn't know what we were talking about either."

"I think you should have made them confess. Maybe one of the sons . . ."

"You take it up with one of the sons if you can find him. You almost married him."

"*Josef?*"

"I didn't even mention it to that shmuck. He doesn't even know which side is up. But it was his mother all the same, believe me, who stole my mother's diamond earrings."

I wanted to tell him that it was wrong to bear a grudge. That it was all over and done with. That you couldn't hold one generation responsible for the sins of another. But it sounded terribly Christian, and I knew my father. It still rankled in his heart. He would never forgive any of them, even Josef.

My father looked around at me. "Go to sleep, *mein kind*, it's late. Did you want to see me about something?"

"How's business, Daddy?" I said.

My father laughed.

"Oh, Daddy!" I cried, throwing my arms around his neck, bursting into tears. "*Daddy, Daddy, Daddy . . .*"

14

Gerald was persistent. I had to say that for him. He pursued me with the same boyish obstinacy he did his tenor lessons. Yet, somehow, now that the way was clear to marry him, the very thought made me ill. Mrs. Lois Muster. The nightmare of the catered affair come true. Now that it was possible, it was impossible. Worst of all, I would one day tell Dr. Hamburger and he would say, "Why are you still calling yourself 'you'?" I took sanctuary for the weekend at Rosalie's house, and Gerald kept calling me there, though I didn't know how many times Rosalie told him I wouldn't come to the phone. He didn't believe I was serious this time. He even made an appointment with my father to meet him down in my father's office at Lowyse Frocks. "Please, Daddy," I said, "I don't want you to talk to him. I never want to see him again." "Are you sure you mean it?" "Definitely." Rosalie didn't think I meant it either, and why should she? We had broken up and reconciled so many times. In fact, I did mean it, though I didn't know why. Mrs. Golden was pretty good about the sudden honor of my company. She skirted around me, avoiding any kind of fraught issue. What she didn't know was what kind of influence I was having on Rosalie, whether I had encouraged her to move in with her boyfriend or not. She went around straightening the objects on the piano top, floated a few extra rosebuds in the centerpiece at dinnertime, told Rosalie to be kind to her kid brother Clifton, and in general left me and Rosalie to our own devices, which meant going to see a movie at the Paradise, *It Happened in Brooklyn,* with Frank Sinatra—had I ever really been in love with Frank Sinatra? and then walking up and down the Grand Concourse in the heat, sicker at heart and more despondent than either of us had been since freshman year.

Then finally it was Monday. I put on Rosalie's pink satin mules and waited for Clifton to get through picking a pimple in the bathroom before I washed and got dressed. The trip to Medaglia was very long on account of having to originate in the Bronx. First the D train at the Grand Concourse, then a change for the F at

Rockefeller Center. At the last Queens stop we got out, books piled to our chins, summer dresses already wilting, and waited on the long line for the bus to Medaglia, shaking and lurching in place until we arrived at the campus. Then a long slow trudge up the hill. Rosalie had another test, naturally, a make-up on the "spectacle of waste" in Shakespeare. I decided to go to the library, a made-over Quonset hut, and the one sure place of not finding Gerald. Oh, Gerald was poison, I knew that. But would they all be queer? Dr. Slavitt wasn't queer, not by a long shot, but he made passes at his students even though he was married. Also, what was the point of teaching books if you only felt superior to the people who wrote them? Another busload of students had arrived, and then another, and now the green campus was swarming with young people going off in all directions: the cafeteria, I saw Leonora and Maria heading for it arm in arm, the softball field, the English Building, the apple orchard, the Science Building, Medaglia Hall. Maybe we were all still mysteries, still ciphers, but at least the others knew where they meant to pass or fail. And wasn't that the point? To repay? Somewhere behind the agricultural high school a cock crowed. "I owe a cock to Asclepius," I thought, and looked around at Rosalie whom once I had confused with Socrates. She was staring at the shimmering silver platter of Manhattan. There was a look on her face I had seen many times before. She was illuminated, she was exultant. She was Rosalie.

"I'll conquer this town," Rosalie said. "I'll conquer this town."

www.ingramcontent.com/pod-product-compliance
Lightning Source LLC
Chambersburg PA
CBHW022208050726
47590CB00002B/690